# TELES
## (The Cynic Teacher)

SOCIETY OF BIBLICAL LITERATURE
TEXTS AND TRANSLATIONS
GRAECO-ROMAN RELIGION SERIES

edited by
Hans Dieter Betz
and
Edward N. O'Neil

Texts and Translations Number 11
Graeco-Roman Religion Number 3

TELES
(The Cynic Teacher)
by
Edward N. O'Neil

SCHOLARS PRESS
Missoula, Montana

*Teles*

# TELES
## (The Cynic Teacher)
by
Edward N. O'Neil

Published by
**SCHOLARS PRESS**
for
**The Society of Biblical Literature**

Distributed by

**SCHOLARS PRESS**
University of Montana
Missoula, Montana 59812

# TELES
## (The Cynic Teacher)

by

Edward N. O'Neil

Library of Congress Cataloging in Publication Data

Teles.
  Teles (the cynic teacher).

  (Graeco-Roman religion series ; no. 3) (Texts and
translations ; no. 11)
  English and Greek.
  Includes bibliographical references and index.
  CONTENTS: On seeming and being.—On self-sufficiency.
—On exile.—A comparison of poverty and wealth.—On
pleasure not being the goal of life [etc.]
  I. Title.  II. Series.  III. Series: Society of
Biblical Literature. Texts and translations ; no. 11.
PA4441.T25A26   183'.4       76-41800
ISBN 0-89130-092-9

        Printed in the United States of America
                1 2 3 4 5
              Printing Department
             University of Montana
            Missoula, Montana 59812

TABLE OF CONTENTS

# PREFACE

This volume began as a simple translation of Teles. Prompted by my comparative study of Plutarch's treatise *On Love of Wealth* and Early Christian Literature and struck by the obvious influence of Cynicism on both, I found myself reading Teles. One thing led to another, and somewhere along the line came the decision to publish a translation.

As each piece received a tentative translation it was submitted to the members of the Corpus Hellenisticum who met twice a month in the Fall and Spring of 1975-1976 at the Institute for Antiquity and Christianity in Claremont. At each meeting we discussed a current project of one of the members. Unfortunately for them, far too many of those evenings were spent on Teles.

In the course of these discussions, so many questions arose about the interpretation of difficult passages that I began to put together more notes than the original plan envisioned and to make changes in Hense's text. The result of these discussions is this volume which is no longer as simple as I had planned.

To every member of the Corpus Hellenisticum I owe a great debt of gratitude. They made those evenings in lovely Claremont the high point of my life, and they saved me from many a blunder in my work on Teles. Two people in particular must not go unnamed: Professors Hans Dieter Betz and Ronald F. Hock. Both of them have shown unfailing tact and patience as they guided my errant steps around one pitfall after another. Those which remain are, of course, my contribution to the volume.

# INTRODUCTION

Teles has little claim to philosophical distinction,
to literary artistry, to originality of any kind.  This
harsh verdict seems to have been made by most people who
have studied Greek philosophy and literature, and with the
usual snobbery that has often stifled classical scholarship over the centuries scholars have ignored Teles and
lavished their attention on the more glamorous authors.
As a result the Telean bibliography is small.

Yet Teles has some claim to fame and deserves more
attention than he has received.  In the first place, despite his frequently naive reasoning, expressed in Greek
that is sometimes tortured and clumsy, he made use of and
quoted the words of older and more important writers.
Among them are Stilpon, the head of the Megarian school in
the fourth century B.C. and, more importantly, the Cynics
Diogenes, Crates and Bion.

The writings of these men have perished except for
references, paraphrases and quotations by later authors.
Thus, to quote Caesar (*Gallic Wars* I. 12), *sive casu sive
consilio deorum immortalium*, Teles' brief pieces, though
often unsatisfactory and even irritating, provide us with
some of the oldest examples of Cynic writing.  This fact
alone is reason enough for us to pay attention to Teles,
but there are others equally cogent.

Even if Teles' compositions are not entirely original,
even if they are sometimes poorly executed, they still
provide us with the earliest examples of the diatribe as
the older Cynics used the form.  In recent years, of
course, some scholars have questioned the origin, nature,
and even the existence of the diatribe as a separate literary genre.  Usener[1] was apparently the first to express
such doubts, and others[2] have followed his lead.  But
whether the compositions which have traditionally been
called diatribes represent a literary genre or whether

they are simply a method and manner of writing, these
little pieces appear to have been current from the time of
Bion, and their style, subject matter and tone exerted an
enormous influence upon every subsequent period of Greek
and Latin literature until and even after the end of antiquity.[3]   And the earliest examples of this tradition appear in the neglected *sermones* of Teles.

A third reason for studying Teles' works is scarcely
less important than the philosophical and literary ones.
Teles represents the common man.  His language, though
sometimes employing technical, or at least regular, terms
of philosophic discussion, is essentially that of the so-
called man on the street.  It is unpretentious, frequently
colloquial, conversational, and just the sort of speech
that one might have heard in the agora or on any street-
corner.

Yet such public places are not the locale for these
discussions.  Rather, we seem to be in a school, and the
language has that friendly, familiar, light and easy-going
tone which a teacher often uses with young students.  Of
course such a locale may be the invention of the author,
but whatever the real situation, the dramatic one called
for colloquial expressions, and that is what we find in
these little pieces.  Or, to put it another way and use an
old cliché (in good Cynic fasion), Teles presents us with
brief slices of life.

The time and place from which these slices have been
taken can be determined only by an analysis of Teles' own
words, for we have no other information about the man.
And, as often happens in such cases, Teles has given us no
precise data.  He knew when and where he was living; he
knew why and for whom he was composing these discussions,
so why include such useless information?  Yet he has furnished us with at least some indication of the time and
location of his writings.

First, the matter of time. In the third selection
(*On Exile*, p. 23) Teles refers to the Chremonidean War
which lasted from 267 to 262 B.C. (cf. note III. 15). He
also refers to the Spartan Hippomedon and his service in
Thrace under Ptolemy Euergetes. Since Ptolemy did not
seize control of Thrace until 243 or 242 B.C., and since
Hippomedon did not leave Sparta until 241, we have an even
later date to consider. Finally, in his discussion of
Hippomedon's service, Teles says ὁ νῦν ἐπὶ Θρᾴκης καθεσταμένος ὑπὸ Πτολεμαίου, so Hippomedon was still in Ptolemy's
service in Thrace, as far as Teles knew when he wrote
these words.

The reference in this same passage to Chremonides and
Glaucon is less precise.[4] Teles refers to them as πάρεδροι
καὶ σύμβουλοι and, if the punctuation of this passage is
correct, they had held these positions recently: ἵνα μὴ τὰ
παλαιά σοι λέγω, ἀλλὰ τὰ καθ᾿ ἡμᾶς. Chremonides appears
to have been an admiral under Ptolemy until about 242 B.C.,
but the terms πάρεδροι and σύμβουλοι seem to refer to ad-
ministrative, rather than military, posts. Is it possible,
then, to see in Teles' use of these terms a reference to
Chremonides' career after 242 B.C. or was he an advisor
before becoming an admiral? Whatever the case, we have a
clear reference in the third selection to events of 242
B.C. or later.

Yet these references help us to date only the one
treatise, for there is a dearth of datable material in the
other pieces. In fact, there is only one clear reference
to a contemporary situation, and it is too vague for us to
identify a date. In IVB (p. 49) appears this sentence:
"For example, in the present war he (i.e. the poor man) is
concerned about nothing but himself, but the rich man is
concerned about others as well." Unfortunately, there is
no way to identify this war, for, like sin among mankind,
war was always rampant in the Greek world, especially in
the third century B.C. Meineke (cf. Hense *ad loc.*)

identified the war as the Chremonidean, but this is pure guess-work. Meineke may be correct, but there is no obvious way either to confirm or to refute the identification. And these few references are all the information we have for dating Teles. We can say only that he was writing in the middle of the third century B.C., as late as 242 B.C. and perhaps just a bit later.[5]

The indications of Teles' city are scarcely more numerous or definite. In the second selection (περὶ αὐταρκείας) there is a reference (line 43) to ὁ παρθενὼν οὗτος, but these are the words of Diogenes and cannot be used to locate Teles. In the third selection (περὶ φυγῆς) the exiled Lycinus is said (p. 23) to have commanded a garrison παρ᾽ ἡμῖν in the service of Antigonus Gonatas. Unfortunately we know nothing about Lycinus beyond what Teles says, so we cannot determine in which city the garrison was located. It could be Athens or Megara, or even Corinth, since Antigonus captured all three cities and imposed garrisons. In Athens, however, he established several garrisons and placed them under one commander,[6] but the words of Teles seem to imply a single garrison, and it is more likely that a smaller city like Megara could have been controlled by a smaller force.

Furthermore, in this passage Teles seems to be citing examples of the fortunes of exiles in different places. Thus he first names the Italian Lycinus and his fortunes in the city where Teles himself lived; then he describes the lot of the Spartan Hippomedon in Thrace and finally the good fortune of the Athenians Glaucon and Chremonides in Egypt: Men from three different places who prospered in three different places. The only locality left unidentified is the city where Lycinus served. It was almost certainly not Corinth, for we have no reason to suppose that Teles had any connection with that city, and, as we have seen, it cannot be Athens.[7] Consequently, the only

logical choice is Megara, and other remarks in this same
selection point to the same conclusion.

A few lines later (p. 25, cf. notes III. 19-20) Teles
refers to a Thesmophorion and a temple of Enyalius. From
the evidence of Thucydides and Pausanias it is clear that
both of these temples were, or at least could have been,
in Megara. Consider also Teles' words a short time later
(p. 31) where he reports with approval the rejoinder of
some Attic exiles who said that they would be buried "in
Megarian soil just like those of the Megarians who were
pious." One can conclude that no Athenian wrote these
words. More likely the author was a Megarian or at least
one addressing a Megarian audience.

The next allusion to locality occurs in IV A (p. 45).
Here the thoughts of an ambitious slave are described: He
longs to be free, but once free he wants more: to own a
slave himself, to own two slaves, to possess property, to
be an Athenian, a magistrate, a king, then like Alexander
to be immortal and, presumably, to be Zeus. In this
steady progress up the ladder of success, the slave hopes
to become an Athenian. As in the earlier allusion to Megarian soil, the slave's thoughts seem more logical, more
appropriate, in the mind of an Athenian. Of course the
prestige of Athens, even in the third century, was such
that the thought could have been expressed by a non-
Athenian,[8] but the probability is great that these words
come from an Athenian. Was that man Teles or some unnamed
source?

A final allusion to locality occurs in the last selection, περὶ ἀπαθείας (line 76). Teles is describing the
reactions of Spartan women to moments of crisis, and he
contrasts the reactions of Athenian women to similar circumstances, to the detriment of the latter. A short time
later, after describing the actions of another Spartan
woman, he exclaims ὅρα εἰ καὶ τῶν παρ' ἡμῖν τις γυναικῶν
τοῦτ' ἂν ποιήσειεν. One can, of course, interpret these

passages in two ways: παρ' ἡμῖν may simply be another way
of referring to the 'Αττική γυνή of the earlier passage,
in which case we have the words of an Athenian writer, or
the phrase may be an implied contrast between Athenian
women and those of another city.  In that case, the women
are almost certainly Megarian.

These are the only clear references and allusions to
a particular city, and the evidence which they supply is
far from decisive.  There are indications that Teles lived
in Athens, but even stronger are the reference to Megara.
Can the question ever be resolved?[9]  Probably not with the
sort of information which we have at present, but there is
one more passage which cannot be ignored in this discussion.  It may provide us with an additional insight into
the matter.

In the περὶ φυγῆς (p. 25) Teles says "In the same way
I have hitherto considered my own land impossible to walk
upon, and I have changed residence and now am settling down
elsewhere."  This statement may be only a traditional ob-
servation, a *topos* of exile-literature, made personal for
rhetorical effect, but it may also contain some autobio-
graphical data.  If the speaker is really Teles and if the
exile is factual, we may have a way out of our dilemma over
his native city.

Teles may be alluding to the fact that he is an exile
from one city now living in another.  But what city has he
left and where has he settled?  The implications are obvious.  He has just referred to the Thesmophorion and the
temple of Enyalius (already discussed above) and in words
that imply his presence in the city where they stood: οὐδὲ
γὰρ νῦν εἰς τὸ Θεσμοφόριον ἐξουσίαν ἔχω, etc.  Therefore,
if our reasoning is accurate and these temples were in Megara, so was Teles when he wrote the περὶ φυγῆς.  And if,
as other allusions indicate, he was in Athens when he
wrote other selections, we are led to the surmise that he
was an Athenian exile who went to live in Megara.

When and why was he exiled?  The times were too tempestuous, the occasions for such a punishment were too
numerous, for us to speak with certainty.  That the exile
occurred before the Chremonidean War is almost assured,
but how much earlier must remain a matter of further speculation.

There is even the possibility that Teles' exile was
voluntary, though the use of the adjective ἄβατον (III.
note 22) certainly implies an involuntary departure.  He
may, like Crates and other Cynics before him, have left
his native city to become a *Wanderprediger* who was either
visiting Megara or residing there temporarily when he composed the περὶ φυγῆς.  In summary, then, Teles lived or at
least flourished in the middle of the third century B.C.
He resided in Megara at least part of the time, though he
may have come there from Athens.[10]

In Megara at least he seems to have conducted a
school of some kind, and it was for his students that he
put together these pastiches of older Cynic writings replete with quotations of and allusions to Diogenes, Crates
and Bion, with at least two references to the Megarian
Stilpon.  And, to tie everything together, Teles added
some of his own thoughts and observations.

The actual extent of his contributions must, of
course, remain a matter of debate.  Most critics who have
studied these pieces, especially those who are the product
of nineteenth century German scholarship with its penchant
for playing the game of *Quellenforschung*, have tended to
reduce Teles' role to a minimum and to see lurking behind
almost every sentence the sentiment of Diogenes, Crates
and especially Bion.[11]  Admittedly the matter is a complicated one, and the absence of a real text of any of
these older authors, or of Teles himself, only adds complications.  Yet, a more balanced and, consequently, less
biased evaluation may very well give more credit to Teles.

No responsible study can, however, elevate him to the
rank of a literary artist or philosophic thinker.  Teles
was a teacher, and, like any teacher preparing for class-
room presentation, he started with his authorities.  He
quoted them; he paraphrased, distilled and otherwise
adapted their sayings to his own needs and to those of his
students.  Rather than demean and malign the man because
he was no Plato or Aristotle or even a Crates or Bion, we
should be grateful that these little diatribes of his have
somehow survived to furnish us with examples of early
Cynic writings and at the same time to give us occasional
glimpses of Greek life in one of the crucial periods of
antiquity.

The story of the survival of Teles' work is as brief
as it is uncertain and unsatisfactory.[12]  At some unknown
time and place an otherwise unknown Theodorus made an epi-
tome of Teles' writings.  Attempts have been made to identify this Theodorus as a Cynic who lived in the first century A.D., a time of revival of Cynicism.  There is ab-
solutely no evidence for or against such a conjecture nor,
given the present state of our information, any way to
prove or disprove it.  The very name Theodorus was so common in all periods of antiquity that it serves as an effective barrier to any investigation.

Our knowledge of Stobaeus is better but far from
satisfactory.  He seems to have lived in the fifth century
A.D., but where he lived is still unknown.  He is the author of an extensive anthology of pagan poets and prose
writers whose excerpts he arranged according to subject
matter.  Today this anthology appears in the form of two
works.  The first, in two books, bears the title Ἐκλογαὶ
φυσικαὶ διαλεκτικαὶ καὶ ἠθικαί; the second, in one book,
is entitled simply ἀνθολόγιον.[13]

The Telean selections are scattered through both
works and appear under the following headings:[14]

| I | ἐκ τῆς Θεοδώρου τῆς Τέλητος ἐπιτομῆς |
| | περὶ τοῦ δοκεῖν καὶ τοῦ εἶναι.[15] |
| II | ἐκ τοῦ Τέλητος περὶ αὐταρκείας |
| III | Τέλητος περὶ φυγῆς |
| IVA | ἐκ τῶν Τέλητος ἐπιτομή[16] |
| IVB | ἐκ τῶν Τέλητος ἐπιτομή[16] |
| V | ἐκ τῶν Τέλητος περὶ τοῦ μὴ εἶναι |
| | τέλος ἡδονήν. |
| VI | ἐκ τῶν Τέλητος περὶ περιστάσεων |
| VII | ἐκ τῶν Τέλητος περὶ ἀπαθείας |

The very wording of these titles show that what we find in
Stobaeus' anthology is at least a series of extracts from
extracts, and the chances are good (if that is the proper
adjective) that more than one other intervening compres-
sion occurred between Teles and Theodorus and between
Theodorus and Stobaeus. So tenuous is the text history of
these little compositions of Teles!

Equally slight, and in many ways equally unsatisfactory, is the history of Telean scholarship.[17] Strictly
speaking, the *Editio Princeps* of Teles is the same as that
of Stobaeus, and the early editions are merely those portions of the Stobaean editions which contain his selections.[18]

The *Editio Princeps* of the *Eclogues* is by G. Canter
(Antwerp, 1575); that of the *Florilegium* is by Franc.
Trincavelli (Venice, 1536).[19] Among the important editions of the *Eclogues* is that of A.H.L. Heeren (Göttingen,
1792-1801); for the *Florilegium* there are editions of
Conrad Gesner[20] (Zürich, 1543; Basle, 1549; Zürich, 1559)
and Thomas Gaisford (Oxford, 1822 and again, 1850). The
first edition of the whole Stobaean corpus seems to be
that of an unnamed editor who published his work at
Geneva in 1609. The next major edition of the whole corpus is that of August Meineke (Leipzig, 1857). And finally came the edition (Berlin, 1884-1895) of Curt Wachsmuth
(who edited the *Eclogues*) and Otto Hense (who edited the

*Florilegium*).  Hense subsequently published a second edition of the *Florilegium* (Berlin, 1909-1912 reprinted 1958), and so in reality the most recent text of all but the first selection of Teles is to be found in Hense's second edition of Stobaeus' *Florilegium*.

Before that, however, and apparently as a kind of πάρεργον, Hense published a separate edition of the eight selections of Teles (Tübingen, 1889).  The revised, second edition appeared in 1909, and it is this work that has become not only the standard edition of Teles, but really the only edition.  It is Hense's text which all scholars cite in their references to Teles, and it is his pagination and line numbers that have furnished the standard method for citation.  And it is this edition that of necessity forms the basis for the present work.[21]

All too frequently a new editor feels that he must justify his own work by attacking previous efforts.  In the case of Hense's edition of Teles there is much that appears wrong, much that appears naive and perhaps preconceived.  The text of these pieces, as it has come down to us, is less than ideal, and this state of affairs presented Hense (and other scholars as well) with a temptation to tamper with the readings.  Too often Hense yielded to temptation and tried to make Teles say what he thought the Greek writer should have said.  As things stand, one may almost say that Hense wrote Teles.  This is the chief criticism which one must level at Hense, but it is a criticism that can be directed at most of the scholars of the nineteenth century, and especially those of Germany.

Yet there is much that is good about the edition. Hense at least attempted to identify the many textual problems and even to solve them.  He frequently succeeded in his attempts.  That he did not always find the right answer only proves that he was human.  Generally speaking, his second edition is good, and, representing as it does the refining of first efforts on an author whom few

scholars bothered even to read, it is an excellent edition.

For that reason, I have been content in my own first
effort to use his text as the basis for the translation
and notes.  The apparatus here lists only those places
where I disagree with Hense or which, for some reason or
other, deserve special attention.  After I have studied
the material more thoroughly and feel more confident both
with the Telean corpus and with the larger body of Cynic
and Stoic writings, perhaps a better text and a comprehen-
sive commentary will be possible.[22]  Until that time, however, here is Hense's text, slightly revised, prolegomena
to a commentary, and the first complete translation in any
modern language.

NOTES TO INTRODUCTION

[1]H. Usener, *Epicurea*, Berlin 1887, p. lxix. See also Christ-Schmid-Stählin, *Geschichte der griechischen Literatur*[7] 2.1[6], Munich 1920, p. 55, note 2.

[2]Eduard Norden, *Antike Kunstprosa*, Leipzig 1898, p. 129, described the diatribe as nothing more than "*ein in die Form der Deklamation umgewandelter Dialog.*" See also H. Rahn, *Morphologie der antiken Literatur, Eine Einführung*, Darmstadt 1969, p. 156. For what it is worth, cf. A. Lesky, *A History of Greek Literature* (translated by J. Willis and C. de Heer), London 1966, pp. 670ff. Lesky assumes that the diatribe is a literary genre and, despite all attempts to disprove this point of view, the burden of proof must remain with those who deny the designation.

[3]In addition to the works already cited, the following are especially important: R. Bultmann, *Der Stil der Paulinischen Predigt und die kynisch-stoische Diatribe*, Göttingen 1910; W. Capelle and H. Marrow, *Reallexikon für Antike und Christentum* (s.v. "Diatribe"); D. R. Dudley, *A History of Cynicism*, London 1937; R. Höistad, *Cynic Hero and Cynic King*, Uppsala 1948; E. G. Schmid, *Der Kleine Pauly* (s.v. "Diatribe"); F. Sayre, *Diogenes of Sinope*, Baltimore 1938; F. Sayre, *The Greek Cynics*, Baltimore 1948; P. Wendland, *Philo und die kynisch-stoische Diatribe*, Berlin 1895.

[4]Our information about Chremonides and Glaucon is scanty, and even what we have is not beyond dispute. The usual items listed, however, in such works as *Der Kleine Pauly* and *Pauly-Wissowa* are these: The two men were brothers, sons of an Athenian named Eteocles of the deme Αἰθαλίδαι. Glaucon, who was older than Chremonides, won a victory in the chariot-race at the Olympian Games in 282/1 B.C. (when Nicias was Archon). On this statue which was set up to commemorate that victory was inscribed ἀγωνοθέτης καὶ στρατηγὸς ἐπὶ τῶν ὅπλων (CIA II.1291). These words may refer to his position in 288 B.C. when Glaucon joined with Olympiodorus to lead the Nationalists in overthrowing the government of Athens when the Egyptian fleet of Ptolemy I appeared off the Piraeus. Although Glaucon probably remained active in Athenian politics during the next twenty years or so, we hear nothing about him until the end of the Chremonidean war.

In the intervening years it was the younger brother Chremonides who became the more prominent. He seems to have been a follower of the philosopher Zeno (who died during the siege of Athens by Antigonus in 263 B.C.), and, if we can believe Diogenes Laertius (VII.17), he was a favorite of Zeno in every sense of the word. In 267 he led the Nationalists in overthrowing the pro-Macedonian

government of Athens and into an alliance with Egypt.  The
result of this action was the so-called Chremonidean war,
which was a disaster for Athens.  (For details of the war,
cf. W. W. Tarn, *Cambridge Ancient History*, vol. VII, ch.
VI, pp. 218ff.; ch. XXII, pp. 705ff.).  Antigonus Gonatas
recaptured Athens and imposed several garrisons.  He seems
not to have ordered executions of the anti-Macedonian
leaders, but some at least went into forced or voluntary
exile.

Among these exiles were Glaucon and Chremonides.  They
fled to Egypt where they became important officials in the
service of Ptolemy II.  In addition to their positions as
πάρεδροι and σύμβουλοι, as Teles describes them (cf. Tarn,
*CAH* VII, p. 29), Glaucon appears to have become a priest
of Alexander in 255 (*CAH* VII, p. 220), and he appears as a
πρόξενος of Rhodes in an inscription (IG ns. I.25).
Chremonides became an admiral of the Egyptian fleet, a
position he held until at least about 242 B.C. when he was
in command of the fleet at Ephesus during the Rhodian seige
of that city (Polyaenus V.18).

[5]G. Droysen (*Hellenismus* III. 1,407ff.) further con-
tends that Teles could not have written the περὶ φυγῆς after 229 B.C.

[6]W. W. Tarn, *CAH* VII, pp. 220f.  Another fact which
points away from Athens is that Antigonus placed an Athenian in charge of the garrison commanders.  The whole point
of Teles' discussion is that Lycinus was a foreigner in
the city which he controlled.

[7]Although it is dangerous to argue from silence, one
can imagine that, if the city had been Athens, Teles could
not have resisted the chance to point out that some men
prospered as exiles in that city while others, like Glaucon
and Chremonides, had to leave in order to win renown.

[8]This is the argument of Hense, p. XXXVIf.

[9]Hense and several others who have investigated the
problem believe that they have indeed resolved the question.  They accept every allusion which points to Megara
as coming from Teles and attribute the Athenian references
to one of his sources.  See Hense, pp. XXXV-XXXIX.  Teles
may indeed be Megarian, but the evidence is far from over-
whelming.

[10]Hense's argument (p. XXXVII) that Teles is a Megarian name is interesting but hardly persuasive.

[11]For a discussion of Teles' sources and his use of
them see Hense, pp. XLIVff.

[12]Cf. Hense, pp. XVff.

[13]For a thorough analysis of Stobaeus' work see
Hense's article in *PW* XX. 2549ff. The standard text is
that of C. Wachsmuth and O. Hense, Berlin 1884-1923.

[14]The Roman numerals are, of course, those used by
Hense in his edition of Teles and retained in the present
volume.

[15]The significance of the fact that Theodorus' name
appears only with the first selection has raised some
questions about Stobaeus' sources. See Hense, pp. XIVff.

[16]On the more complete title of IVA and IVB, see note
IVA. 1.

[17]Individual passages of Teles are of course discussed in the volumes on Cynicism which are listed above,
but so few are the individual studies on some passage or
aspect of this material that the bibliography can be listed here in one brief note:

Barigazzi, A.: "Note al De exilio di Telete e di
Musonio," *SIFC* XXXIV (1962), pp. 70-82.

Capelle, W.: *Epiktet, Teles und Musonius, Wege zu
glückseligem Leben*, Zürich 1948.

Diels, H.: *"Teles apud Stobaei florilegium,"
Hermes* 13 (1879), pp. 1-9.

Fuks, A.: "Non-Phylarchan Tradition of the Pro-
gramme of Agis IV" *CQ* XII (1962), pp.
118-121. A discussion of Teles III.

Giesecke, A.: *De philosophorum veterum quae ad
exilium spectant sententiis*, Diss.
Inaug., Leipzig, 1891. A discussion
of Teles III.

Gigante, M.: "Il filo del mantello" *PP* XXIV (1969),
pp. 214-216.

Mueller, H.: *De Teletis elocutione*, Diss. Inaug.,
Freiburg im Breisgau, 1891.

Musso, O.: "Telete e la battaglia di Efeso," *PP*
XVII (1962), pp. 129-131.

Süpfle, G.: "Ist der Cyniker Teles mit Recht als
der älteste Vorfahr des geistlichen
Redners bezeichnet worden?" in *Zur Geschichte der cynischen Secte, Archiv
für Geschichte der Philosophie* 4
(1891), pp. 414-423.

[18]Teles appears in Stobaeus as follows: I: *Eclogues*
II. 15, 47. The rest are in the *Florilegium*: II: III. 1,
98; III: III. 40, 8; IVA: IV. 33, 31; IVB: IV. 32ᵃ, 21;
V: IV. 34, 72; VI: IV. 44, 82; VII: IV. 44, 83.

[19]For information on the text history of Stobaeus,
see J. E. Sandys, *A History of Classical Scholarship*, New
York 1958, and Wachsmuth-Hense, vol. 1, pp. xxivff.

[20]Gesner has created a minor problem for those who
are interested in Teles. He assigned to Teles two anony-
mous selections in Stobaeus (*Flor.* IV. 91, 34 and IV. 93,
84 in Hense's text) which have the same title: Ἐκ τοῦ
περὶ συγκρίσεως πλούτου καὶ ἀρετῆς. Others, however, have
now rejected Telean authorship and supported their objec-
tions with proof. Among them are Wilamowitz (*Antigonus
von Karystos*, Berlin 1881, Excursus III, pp. 292ff.),
Meineke (in his edition of Stobaeus), and Hense himself
(in his edition of Teles, pp. XVIIff.).

These men were right in rejecting Telean authorship,
for neither the subject matter nor the style of either
piece even remotely resembles that of Teles. Indeed, there
is little in either that accords with Cynic thought. Furthermore, the style and, despite the identical titles, the
subject matter and point of view in them is so different
that one can only conclude that the same man did not write
both.

The author of the first piece has made no pretense at
literary artistry. The style is simple, the language
straightforward and plain. On the other hand, the style
of the second is often pretentious and tortured while the
language is difficult and obscure, thereby frequently
failing to yield adequate sense. But, whether or not the
same man wrote both pieces, neither can be attributed to
Teles.

The first selection contains a defense of wealth,
with the greater portion delivered by Wealth himself, who
claims that all the good things in this world, both spiri-
tual and material, come from him. In his defense Wealth
manages to use or to convert many of the clichés that are
a standard part of the literature on wealth.

The second selection, which at times almost seems to
be the thoughts of Wealth's prosecutor (without the dramatic situation in the other selection), presents the opposite side of the argument. It is an attack on Wealth who
"has countless drugs for evil" and who brings mankind most
of its woes. There is a list of the problems that Wealth
brings and another list of the woes that a wealthy man
must endure.

All of this, in summary at least, sounds like the
sort of thing a Cynic might say, but there is a difference.
There is no praise of self-sufficiency, of contentment
with one's lot. There are no similes such as we have
learned to expect in Cynic compositions, no references to
Socrates or Diogenes, Crates or Bion. Some of the thoughts
and expressions may be Stoic, but few, if any, can be
Cynic. Yet the two selections are not without interest and
deserve more investigation.

[21]This is perhaps the place to explain the numbering
system used in this volume. The number which Hense used
for each selection has been retained. Here, however, the

lines in each piece are numbered consecutively and appear
in the right margin.  In the left margin of both the text
and the translation the page number of Hense's text is in-
serted at the proper place.  This number is followed by
the letter "H," and the whole citation is put in parentheses, e.g. (33H).  In this way, the reader can easily find
the same passage in Hense's edition.

[22]And hopefully colleagues will, with their reviews
and criticism of this first effort, provide a firmer base
for future study.

TEXT AND TRANSLATION

2

(3Η)   Περὶ τοῦ δοκεῖν καὶ τοῦ εἶναι

Κρεῖττόν φασι τὸ δοκεῖν δίκαιον εἶναι
τοῦ εἶναι· μὴ καὶ τὸ δοκεῖν ἀγαθὸν εἶναι τοῦ
εἶναι κρεῖττόν ἐστιν;
   Ἀμέλει.
   Πότερον οὖν διὰ τὸ δοκεῖν ἀγαθοὶ ὑποκρι-    5
ταὶ εἶναι <εὖ> ὑποκρίνονται ἢ διὰ τὸ εἶναι;
   <Διὰ τὸ εἶναι.>
   Κιθαρίζουσι δ'<εὖ> πότερον διὰ τὸ δοκεῖν
ἀγαθοὶ κιθαρισταὶ <εἶναι> ἢ διὰ τὸ εἶναι;
   Διὰ τὸ εἶναι.    10
   Τὰ δ'ἄλλα πάντα ἁπλῶς διὰ τὸ δοκεῖν
ἀγαθοὶ <εἶναι> εὖ πράττουσιν ἢ διὰ τὸ εἶναι;
   Διὰ τὸ εἶναι.
   Δι' ὃ δ'εὖ βιοῦσι κρεῖττον ἢ δι' ὃ μή·
ὥστε κρεῖττον φαίνοιτ' ἂν τὸ ἀγαθὸν εἶναι τοῦ    15.
δοκεῖν, ὁ γὰρ δίκαιος ἀγαθός, οὐχ ὁ δοκῶν
δίκαιος εἶναι. καὶ τί ποτε ἐπὶ τῶν ἄλλων
ἀγαθῶν, ὅσα δοκοῦσιν ἄνθρωποι; μᾶλλον ἂν
βούλοιο εἶναι ἐν αὑτοῖς <ἢ δοκεῖν εἶναι> καὶ
ἔχειν αὐτὰ μᾶλλον ἢ δοκεῖν ἔχειν; εὐθέως, ὁρᾶν    20
(4Η)   <μᾶλλον> / ἂν βούλοιο ἢ δοκεῖν ὁρᾶν; ὑγιαίνειν μᾶλλον ἢ δοκεῖν; ἰσχύειν μᾶλλον ἢ δοκεῖν;
εὔπορος εἶναι, φίλους ἔχειν μᾶλλον ἢ δοκεῖν;
ἐπὶ τῶν ψυχικῶν πάλιν, φρονεῖν μᾶλλον ἢ δοκεῖν;
ἄλυπος εἶναι μᾶλλον ἢ δοκεῖν; θαρσαλέος εἶναι,    25
ἄφοβος εἶναι, ἀνδρεῖος εἶναι μᾶλλον ἢ δοκεῖν;
ἐπὶ τῆς δικαιοσύνης δὲ οὐκέτι δίκαιος εἶναι
μᾶλλον ἢ δοκεῖν;
   Ἀλλὰ καὶ ἀνδρεῖος ἂν μᾶλλον βουλοίμην
δοκεῖν ἢ εἶναι.    30

## I

(3H)                    On Seeming and Being

People say that seeming to be just is better
than being so.[1]  Seeming to be good isn't better
than being so, is it?

Certainly not.

Well then, do men act well on the stage because they seem to be good actors or because they
are?

Because they are.

And do men play the cithara well because they
seem to be good cithara players or because they are?

Because they are.

And, generally speaking, do men prosper in all
other matters because they seem to be good or because they are?

Because they are.

And the way by which men choose to live well
is better than the way they reject.[2]  Therefore,
being good would appear better than seeming so, for
the just man is good, not the one who seems to be
just.  And what, then, in the case of other things
which men consider goods?[3]  Would you rather be
engaged in their pursuit or seem to be, and to
possess them rather than seem to possess them?  For
(4H)    example, would you rather see or seem to see?  To
be healthy rather than to seem so?  To be wealthy,
to have friends rather than to seem so?  Again, in
the matter of the goods of the soul, to be intelligent rather than to seem so?  To have peace of mind
rather than to seem so?  To be confident, to be
fearless, to be courageous rather than to seem so?[4]
Yet in the matter of justice, no longer to be just
rather than to seem so?

Well, I would rather seem courageous than to
be so.

᾽Η οὐχ ὁ ἀνδρεῖος καὶ ἄφοβος καὶ ἄλυπος, οὐχ
ὁ δοκῶν; διὰ τί δὲ βούλει ἀνδρεῖος δοκεῖν εἶναι;
   Τιμήσουσί με.
   Καὶ γὰρ πρωτοστάτην σε καταστήσουσι καὶ
μονομαχεῖν κελεύσουσι καὶ ἵνα λάχῃς μηχανήσονται   35
καὶ λαχόντι σοι ἐπιχαρήσονται καθάπερ τῷ Αἴαντι·
εἶτα τί οἴει πείσεσθαι δειλὸς μὲν ὤν, κινδυνεύων
δέ; καὶ ἐὰν αἰχμάλωτος γένῃ δοκῶν ἀνδρεῖος εἶναι
πέδας ἕξεις μεγάλας καὶ χειροπέδας, καὶ οὐθείς
σοι μὴ πιστεύσει, ἀλλὰ καὶ κατακεκλεισμένος        40
ἔσῃ, κἂν βασανίζωσί σε πολλὰς λήψῃ, καὶ λέγων
τὴν ἀλήθειαν οὐ μὴ πιστευθήσῃ, ἀλλὰ δόξεις
μωκᾶσθαι διὰ τὸ δοκεῖν καρτερικὸς εἶναι, καὶ
κελεύσουσί σε δέρειν καὶ ἐπιτείνειν καὶ παροπ-
τᾶν.  ὅρα πόσα λήψῃ δοκῶν ἀνδρεῖος εἶναι καὶ     45
καρτερικός· σὺ δὲ ἐκεῖνο μὲν προφέρῃ, ταῦτα
δὲ ἀποκρύπτεις, ὥσπερ οἱ ῥήτορες.

Isn't the courageous man also fearless and undisturbed, not the one who seems so?  Why do you want to seem courageous?

People will honor me.

Yes indeed, and they will station you as the first man on the right side of the battle line[5] and will order you to engage in single combat.  They will contrive for your lot to be drawn and when it has been drawn they will gloat over you just as they did over Ajax.[6]  Then what do you think you'll experience, since you are a coward and in danger?  And if you become a prisoner, since you seem to be courageous, you'll wear huge shackles and handcuffs, and no one will trust you.  Why, you'll even be locked up, and if they torture you, you will receive many blows.  And even when you tell the truth, you will not be believed.  Instead, you will seem to be mocking them on account of seeming to have endurance, and they will order you to be beaten and stretched on the rack and roasted.  See how many things you will receive by seeming to be courageous and capable of endurance?  But you put that up as a front, and conceal these things, like the politicians.[7]

## II

Περὶ αὐταρκείας

Δεῖ ὥσπερ τὸν ἀγαθὸν ὑποκριτὴν ὃ τι ἂν ὁ
ποιητὴς περιθῇ πρόσωπον τοῦτο ἀγωνίζεσθαι καλῶς,
οὕτω καὶ τὸν ἀγαθὸν ἄνδρα ὃ τι ἂν περιθῇ ἡ τύχη.
καὶ γὰρ αὕτη, φησὶν ὁ Βίων, ὥσπερ ποιήτρια, ὁτὲ
μὲν πρωτολόγου, ὁτὲ δὲ δευτερολόγου περιτίθησι          5
πρόσωπον, καὶ ὁτὲ μὲν βασιλέως, ὁτὲ δὲ ἀλήτου.
μὴ οὖν βούλου δευτερολόγος ὢν τὸ πρωτολόγου
πρόσοπον· εἰ δὲ μή, / ἀναρμοστόν τι ποιήσεις.

Σὺ μὲν ἄρχεις καλῶς, ἐγὼ δὲ ἄρχομαι, φησί,
καὶ σὺ μὲν πολλῶν, ἐγὼ δὲ ἑνὸς τουτουῖ παι-          10
δαγωγὸς γενόμενος, καὶ σὺ μὲν εὔπορος γενόμενος
δίδως ἐλευθερίως, ἐγὼ δὲ λαμβάνω εὐθαρσῶς παρὰ
σοῦ οὐχ ὑποπίπτων οὐδὲ ἀγεννίζων οὐδὲ μεμψι-
μοιρῶν. σὺ κέχρασαι τοῖς πολλοῖς καλῶς, ἐγὼ
δὲ τοῖς ὀλίγοις· οὐ γὰρ τὰ πολυτελῆ, φησί,          15
τρέφει, οὐδὲ ἐκείνοις μὲν ἔστι μετ' ὠφελείας
χρῆσθαι, τοῖς δὲ ὀλίγοις καὶ εὐτελέσι μετὰ
σωφροσύνης [οὐκ] ἔστι καὶ ἀτυφίας.

Διὸ καὶ εἰ λάβοι, φησὶν ὁ Βίων, φωνὴν τὰ
πράγματα, ὃν τρόπον καὶ ἡμεῖς, καὶ δύναιτο          20
δικαιολογεῖσθαι, οὐκ ἂν εἴποι, [φησίν, πρῶτον
ἡ πενία, 'ἄνθρωπε, τί μοι μάχη';] ὥσπερ οἰκέτης
πρὸς τὸν κύριον ἐφ' ἱερὸν καθίσας δικαιολογεῖται
'τί μοι μάχη; μή τί σοι κέκλοφα; οὐ πᾶν τὸ
προσταττόμενον ὑπὸ / σου ποιῶ; οὐ τὴν ἀποφορὰν          25
εὐτάκτως σοι φέρω;' καὶ ἡ Πενία <ἂν> εἴποι πρὸς
τὸν ἐγκαλοῦντα 'τί μοι μάχη; μὴ καλοῦ τινος δι'
ἐμὲ στερίσκη; μὴ σωφροσύνης; μὴ δικαιοσύνης;

---

18:  οὐκ deleted by ENO.   20-21: φησίν deleted by ENO;
πρῶτον...μάχη deleted by Wilamowitz.

## II

### On Self-Sufficiency

Just as a good actor must perform properly whatever role the poet assigns him, so too must a good man perform whatever Dame Fortune assigns.[1]

For she, says Bion, like a poetess,[2] sometimes assigns the role of first-speaker, sometimes that of second-speaker; and sometimes that of king, sometimes that of a vagabond. Do not, therefore, want the role of first-speaker when you are a second-

(6H) speaker.[3] Otherwise you will commit some discordant act.

You rule properly, and I obey, he says;[4] and you are the leader of many, but I of this one alone; and you, since you are wealthy, give freely, but I receive from you confidently, not submissively or like a low-born man or with grumbling. You enjoy many things properly, but I just a few. For it is not expensive things, he says, that nourish, nor is it possible to use them with profit, but it is [not] possible to use the few and the inexpensive with self-control[5] and moderation.

Therefore, if affairs could acquire a voice, says Bion, in the same way as we, and could plead their case, would they not speak [Poverty first says, "fellow, why do you fight me?"] as a steward would plead to his master after sitting down in a

(7H) sanctuary: "Why do you fight me? I haven't cheated you out of anything, have I? Don't I do everything you command?[6] Don't I regularly pay you a share of my earnings?" And Poverty would say to the man who complains, "Why do you fight me? You aren't being deprived of any good because of me are you? Not of wisdom, are you? Not of justice, not of courage?

&lt;μὴ&gt; ἀγδρείας; ἀλλὰ μὴ τῶν ἀναγκαίων ἐνδεὴς εἶ;
ἢ οὐ μεσταὶ μὲν αἱ ὁδοὶ λαχάνων, πλήρεις δὲ αἱ          30
κρῆναι ὕδατος; οὔκ εὐνάς σοι τοσαύτας παρέχω
ὁπόση γῆ; καὶ στρωμνὰς φύλλα; ἢ εὐφραίνεσθαι
μετ' ἐμοῦ οὐκ ἔστιν; ἢ οὐχ ὁρᾷς γράδια φυστὴν
φαγόντα τερετίζοντα; ἢ οὐκ ὄψον ἀδάπανον καὶ
ἀτρύφερον παρασκευάζω σοι τὴν πεῖναν; ἢ οὐχ ὁ          35
πεινῶν ἥδιστα ἐσθίει καὶ ἥκιστα ὄψου δεῖται;
καὶ ὁ διψῶν ἥδιστα πίνει καὶ ἥκιστα τὸ μὴ

(8H)    παρὸν ποτὸν ἀναμένει; ἢ πεινᾷ τις πλα/κοῦντα
ἢ διψᾷ Χῖον; ἀλλ' οὐ ταῦτα διὰ τρυφὴν ζητοῦσιν
ἄνθρωπος; ἢ οἰκήσεις οὐ παρέχω σοι προῖκα, τὸν          40
μὲν χειμῶνα τὰ βαλανεῖα, θέρους δὲ τὰ ἱερά;
ποῖον γάρ σοι τοιοῦτον οἰκητήριον, φησὶν ὁ
Διογένης, τοῦ θέρους, οἷον ἐμοὶ ὁ παρθενὼν
οὗτος, εὔπνους καὶ πολυτελής';

    Εἰ ταῦτα λέγοι ἡ Πενία, τί ἂν ἔχοις          45
ἀντειπεῖν; ἐγὼ μὲν γὰρ &lt;ἂν&gt; δοκῶ ἄφωνος
γενέσθαι. ἀλλ' ἡμεῖς πάντα μᾶλλον ἀντιώμεθα
ἢ τὴν ἑαυτῶν δυστροπίαν καὶ κακοδαιμονίαν, τὸ
γῆρας, τὴν πενίαν, τὸν ἀπαντήσαντα, τὴν ἡμέραν,
τὴν ὥραν, τὸν τόπον. διὸ φησιν ὁ Διογένης          50
φωνῆς ἀκηκοέναι κακίας ἑαυτὴν αἰτιωμένης,

        οὔτις ἐμοὶ τῶνδ'ἄλλος ἐπαίτιος, ἀλλ'ἐγὼ
                                        αὐτή.

(9H)    παράφοροι δὲ πολλοὶ οὐχ ἑαυτοῖς  ἀλλὰ
τοῖς πράγμασι τὴν αἰτίαν ἐπάγουσιν.  ὁ          55
δὲ Βίων, ὥσπερ τῶν θηρίων, φησί, παρὰ τὴν
λῆψιν ἡ δῆξις γίνεται, κἂν μέσου τοῦ ὄφεως
ἐπιλαμβάνῃ, δηχθήσῃ, ἐὰν τοῦ τραχήλου, οὐδὲν
πείσῃ· οὕτω καὶ τῶν πραγμάτων, φησί, παρὰ τὴν
ὑπόληψιν ἡ ὀδύνη γίνεται, καὶ ἐὰν μὲν οὕτως          60
ὑπολάβῃς περὶ αὐτῶν, ὡς ὁ Σωκράτης, οὐκ
ὀδυνήσῃ, ἐὰν δὲ ὡς ἑτέρως, ἀνιάσῃ, οὐχ ὑπὸ

Well, you aren't in want of the necessities, are
you?  Or aren't the roads full of vegetables and
the springs overflowing with water?  Don't I offer
you such beds as the earth affords and the leaves
for mattresses?  Or isn't it possible to find en-
joyment with me?  Or don't you see old hags eating
a coarse barley-cake[7] and chirping away?  Or don't
I provide you with an inexpensive and simple sauce,
your hunger?  Or isn't it true that a hungry man
most enjoys eating and least misses the sauce?[8]
And the thirsty man most enjoys drinking and least

(8H)     awaits the drink that is not at hand?  Or does anyone hunger for cake or thirst for Chian?  But don't
men seek these things because of luxury?  Or don't
I offer you shelter free of charge: in winter the
baths, in summer the sanctuaries?[9]  'For what sort
of dwelling do you have in summer,' says Diogenes,
'such as I have in this chamger of the Parthenon,[10]
airy and expensive?'"

     If Poverty should say these things to you,
what would you have to say in return?  As for me, I
think I would be mute.  Indeed, we put the blame on
everything rather than our own stubborn character
and unhappiness: on old age, poverty, the one we
chance to meet, the day, the hour, the place.[11]
Wherefore Diogenes says that he has heard the voice
of Wickedness accusing herself:[12]

     None else caused me these things, just I
                              myself.

(9H)     Yet many misguided men lay the blame, not on
themselves, but on circumstances.  And Bion says
that just as in the taking[13] of wild beasts biting
occurs, and if you take hold of a snake by the middle, you will be bitten, but if by the neck you will
suffer no harm, so too in circumstances, he says.
With the wrong assumption[14] of them pain occurs,
and if you have the same understanding of them as
Socrates, you will feel no pain, but if in any

τῶν πραγμάτων ἀλλ' ὑπὸ τῶν ἰδίων τρόπων καὶ
τῆς ψευδοῦς δόξης.

    Διὸ δεῖ μὴ τὰ πράγματα πειρᾶσθαι μετατιθέ-   65
(10H)  ναι, ἀλλ' / αὐτὸν παρασκευάζειν πρὸς ταῦτά πως
ἔχοντα, ὅπερ ποιοῦσιν οἱ ναυτικοί· οὐ γὰρ τοὺς
ἀνέμους καὶ τὴν θάλατταν πειρῶνται μετατιθέναι,
ἀλλὰ παρασκευάζουσιν αὐτοὺς δυναμένους πρὸς
ἐκεῖνα στρέφεσθαι. εὐδία, γαλήνη· ταῖς κώπαις   70
πλέουσι. κατὰ ναῦν ἄνεμος· ἐπῆραν τὰ ἄρμενα.
ἀντιπέπνευκεν· ἐστείλαντο, μεθεῖντο. καὶ σὺ
πρὸς τὰ παρόντα <ὅρα,> χρῶ. γέρων γέγονας· μὴ
ζήτει τὰ τοῦ νέου. ἀσθενὴς πάλιν· μὴ ζήτει τὰ
τοῦ ἰσχυροῦ φορτία βαστάζειν καὶ διατραχηλίζεσ-   75
θαι, ἀλλ' ὥσπερ Διογένης, ἐπεί τις ὤθει καὶ
ἐτραχήλιζεν ἀσθενῶς ἔχοντα, οὐ διετραχηλίζετο,
(11H)  ἀλλὰ δείξας αὐτῷ / τὸν κίονα 'βέλτιστε' φησί
'τοῦτον ὤθει προσστάς.' ἄπορος πάλιν γέγονας·
μὴ ζήτει τὴν τοῦ εὐπόρου δίαιταν, ἀλλ' ὡς πρὸς   80
τὸν ἀέρα φράττῃ (εὐδία, [καὶ] διεστείλω· ψῦχος,
συνεστείλω), οὕτω καὶ πρὸς τὰ ὑπάρχοντα· εὐπο-
ρία, διάστειλον· ἀπορία, σύστειλον. ἀλλ' ἡμεῖς
οὐ δυνάμεθα ἀρκεῖσθαι τοῖς παροῦσιν, ὅταν καὶ
τρυφῇ πολὺ διδῶμεν, καὶ τὸ ἐργάζεσθαι <συμφο-   85
ρὰν> κρίνωμεν καὶ τὸν θάνατον ἔσχατον [τι] τῶν
κακῶν. ἐὰν δὲ ποιήσῃ καὶ τῆς ἡδονῆς καταφρο-
νοῦντά τινα, καὶ πρὸς τοὺς πόνους μὴ διαβεβλη-
μένον, καὶ πρὸς δόξαν καὶ ἀδοξίαν ἴσως ἔχοντα,
καὶ τὸν θάνατον μὴ φοβούμενον, ὅ τι ἂν θέλῃς   90
ἐξέσται σοι ἀνωδύνῳ ὄντι ποιεῖν. διὸ ἅπερ
(12H)  λέγω, / οὐχ ὁρῶ πῶς αὐτὰ

---

72:  μεθεῖντο ENO] μεθείλαντο mss. See note 17.
73:  ὅρα suggested by Buecheler. See Hense's apparatus.
75:  φορτία...διατραχηλίζεσθαι deleted by Wilamowitz, fol-
     lowed by Hense, unnecessarily.
85:  συμφορὰν suggested but not printed by Hense.

other way, you will be distressed, not by circumstances, but by your own character and false opinion.[15]

(10H)
Therefore one should not try to change circumstances, but rather to prepare oneself for them as
they are, just as sailors do. For they do not try
to change the winds and the sea,[16] but instead they
prepare themselves to be able to cope with those
things. There is fair weather, a calm sea: They
propel the ship with oars. The wind is with the
ship: they hoist the sails. It blows contrary:
they furl the sails, they give the ship its way.[17]
And as for you, <regard> your present situation,
use it.[18] You have grown old: do not seek the
things of a young man. Again, you have become
weak: do not seek to carry and submit your neck to
the loads of a strong man.[19] But just as Diogenes,
when someone was shoving him and twisting his neck
when he was indisposed, did not submit but instead

(11H)
showed the fellow his penis,[20] and says, "My dear
sir, stand here in front of me and shove on this."
Again, you have become destitute: do not seek the
rich man's way of life, but as you protect yourself
against the air (fair weather: you throw open your
clothes; cold: you wrap them around you), so also
toward possessions: prosperity: loosen up; scarcity:
tighten up.[21] But we cannot be satisfied with our
present lot when we pay too much attention to luxury and consider work <a disaster> and death the
worst of evils. But if you consider yourself as
one who looks down on pleasure, as one who does not
discredit hard work, and as one who holds good and
bad reputation as equal, and as one who does not
fear death, it will be possible for you to do whatever you want without distress. Therefore, as I

12

τὰ πράγματα ἔχει τι δύσκολον, ἢ γῆρας ἢ πενία
ἢ ξενία. οὐκ ἀηδῶς γὰρ Ξενοφῶν 'ἐάν σοι' φησί
'δείξω δυὸ ἀδελφῶν τὴν ἴσην οὐσίαν διελομένων      95
τὸν μὲν ἐν τῇ πάσῃ ἀπορίᾳ, τὸν δὲ ἐν εὐκολίᾳ,
οὐ φανερὸν ὅτι οὐ τὰ χρήματα αἰτιατέον ἀλλ'
ἕτερόν τι;' οὕτως ἐάν σοι δείξω δύο γέροντας,
δύο πένητας, δύο φεύγοντας, τὸν μὲν ἐν τῇ πάσῃ
εὐκολίᾳ καὶ ἀπαθείᾳ ὄντα, τὸν δὲ ἐν τῇ πάσῃ      100
ταραχῇ, οὐ φανερὸν ὅτι οὐ τὸ γῆρας, οὐ τὴν
πενίαν, οὐ τὴν ξενίαν αἰτιατέον ἀλλ' ἕτερόν
τι;

  Καὶ ὅπερ Διογένης ἐποίησεν πρὸς τὸν
πολυτελῆ φάμενον πόλιν εἶναι τὰς Ἀθήνας...      105
(13H) λαβὼν γὰρ αὐτὸν ἦγεν / εἰς τὸ μυροπωλεῖον καὶ
ἐπυνθάνετο πόσου τῆς κύπρου ἡ κοτύλη. ᾿μνᾶς
φησὶν ὁ μυροπώλης᾿ ἀνέκραγε 'πολυτελής γε ἡ
πόλις.' ἀπῆγεν αὐτὸν πάλιν εἰς τὸ μαγειρεῖον
καὶ ἐπυνθάνετο πόσου τὸ ἀκροκώλιον. 'τριῶν      110
δραχμῶν'᾿ ἐβόα 'πολυτελής γε ἡ πόλις.' εἰς τὰ
ἔρια πάλιν τὰ μαλακὰ καὶ 'πόσου τὸ πρόβατον;'
'μνᾶς' φησίν᾿ ἐβόα 'πολυτελής γε ἡ πολις'.
'δεῦρο δή' φησί. κἀνταῦθα ἄγει αὐτὸν καὶ εἰς
τοὺς θέρμους. 'πόσου ἡ χοῖνιξ;' 'χαλκοῦ'      115
φησίν᾿ ἀνέκραγεν ὁ Διογένης 'εὐτελής γε ἡ
πολις'. πάλιν εἰς τὰς ἰσχάδας, 'δύο χαλκῶν'.
'τῶν δὲ μύρτων;' 'δύο χαλκῶν'᾿ 'εὐτελής γε ἡ
πόλις'. ὃν τρόπον οὖν ὧδε οὐχ ἡ πόλις εὐτελης
καὶ <πολυτελής, ἀλλ' ἐάν μέν τις οὕτω ζῇ,>      120
πολυτελής, ἐὰν δὲ οὕτως, εὐτελής, οὕτω καὶ τὰ
πράγματα, ἐὰν μὲν αὐτοῖς οὕτω χρῆται, εὐπετῆ
καὶ ῥᾴδια φανεῖται, ἐὰν δὲ οὕτως, δυσχερῆ.

---

105:  There is probably a lacuna here. See note 24.
112:  'πόσου τὸ πρόβατον;' punctuated by ENO]
   πόσου τὸ προβατον. Hense.

(12H)   say, I do not see how circumstances themselves have anything troublesome, not old age or poverty or lack of citizenship. For not ineptly does Xenophon say,[22] "If I show you two brothers who have divided an equal sum, one of whom is in utter distress while the other is quite content, isn't it obvious that the money is not to be blamed but something else?" So if I show you two old men, two poor men, two exiles, one of whom is quite content and tranquil while the other is in total turmoil, isn't it obvious that it is not old age, not poverty, not lack of citizenship that should be blamed but something else?

      And just as Diogenes[23] did to the man who said

(13H)   that Athens was an expensive city . . . .[24] For he took him and led him to the perfumer's shop and asked the price of a half-pint of Kypros.[25] "A mina," said the perfumer; he cried out, "The city is indeed expensive!" He led him again to the meat-market and asked the price of trotters, "Three drachmas." He shouted, "The city is indeed expensive!" Forward again to the soft wools and "how much are the sheep?" "A mina," he says. He shouted, "The city is indeed expensive!" "Come on," he says, and at that point led him to the lupine market. "How much for a peck?"[26] "A copper," he says. Diogenes cried out, "The city is indeed inexpensive!" Again he led him to the dried figs, "two coppers"; "the myrtle?" "Two coppers," "The city is indeed inexpensive!" So in this way, as you see, it is not the city that is inexpensive <and expensive, but only if a person lives in this fashion is it expensive, or if he lives so,> is it inexpensive. So, too, with circumstances: if one uses them in one way, they appear trouble-free and easy, but if he uses them in another way, they appear difficult.

14

(14H)      'Αλλ' ὅμως δοκεῖ μοι ἔχειν τι ἡ / πενία
δυσχερὲς καὶ ἐπίπονον· καὶ μᾶλλον ἄν τις          125
ἐπαινέσαι τὸν μετὰ πενίας εὐκόλως <τὸ> γῆρας
ἐνεγκόντα ἢ τὸν μετὰ πλούτου.

           Καὶ τί ἔχει δυσχερὲς ἢ ἐπίπονον ἡ πενία;
ἢ οὐ Κράτης καὶ Διογένης πένητες ἦσαν; καὶ πῶς
<οὐ> ῥᾳδίως διεξήγαγον, ἄτυφοι γενόμενοι καὶ          130
ἐπαῖται καὶ διαίτῃ εὐτελεῖ καὶ λιτῇ δυνάμενοι
χρήσασθαι; ἀπορία καὶ δάνεια περιέστηκεν·

(15H)  κόγχον καὶ κύαμον συνάγαγε, φησὶν ὁ / Κράτης,
καὶ τὰ τούτοις πρόσφορα· κἂν τάδε δράσῃς,
ῥᾳδίως στήσεις τρόπαιον κατὰ πενίας. ἢ τί          135
δεῖ μᾶλλον ἐπαινέσαι τὸν μετὰ πενίας εὐκόλως
<τὸ> γῆρας ἐνεγκόντα ἢ τὸν μετὰ πλούτου; ἐπεί
τοι οὐδὲ γνῶναι ῥᾳδιέστερόν ἐστι, ποῖόν τι
ἐστὶ πλοῦτος ἢ ποῖόν τι πενία· ἀλλὰ καὶ πλούτῳ
πολλοὶ μετὰ γήρως δυσκόλως χρῶνται καὶ πενίᾳ          140
ἀγεννῶς καὶ ὀδυρτικῶς· καὶ οὔτε τούτῳ ῥᾴδιον,
ὥστε τῷ πλούτῳ ἐλευθερίως καὶ ἀφόρτως, οὔτε
ἐκείνῳ, ὥστε <τῇ> πενίᾳ γενναίως, ἀλλὰ τοῦ
αὐτοῦ ἀμφότερα, καὶ ὅσπερ τοῖς πολλοῖς δύναται
κατὰ τρόπον, οὗτος καὶ τοῖς ἀνάπαλιν.          145

           Καὶ ἐὰν μὲν ἐκποιῇ πενητεύουσι <δεῖ>
μένειν ἐν τῷ βίῳ, εἰ δὲ μή, ῥᾳδίως ἀπαλλάτ-
τεσθαι ὥσπερ ἐκ πανηγύρεως [οὕτω καὶ ἐκ τοῦ
βίου]. 'καθάπερ καὶ ἐξ οἰκίας,' φησὶν ὁ Βίων,
'ἐξοικιζόμεθα, ὅταν τὸ ἐνοίκιον ὁ μισθώσας οὐ          150
κομιζόμενος τὴν θύραν ἀφέλῃ, τὸν κέραμον ἀφέλῃ,
τὸ φρέαρ ἐγκλείσῃ, οὕτω,' φησί,

(14H)     But still it seems to me that poverty has
something annoying and wearisome in it; and one
would be more inclined to praise the man who contentedly bore old age with poverty than the one who
did so with wealth.

          And what annoyance or discomfort does poverty
possess?  Or weren't Crates and Diogenes poor?[27]
And surely they easily managed to carry on, once
they became moderate, beggars, and able to enjoy a
way of life that was inexpensive and frugal.  "Scarcity and debts abound: collect shell and bean,"
(15H)   says Crates, "and things appropriate to these;[28]
and if you do this, you will easily set up a
trophy over poverty."  Or why must we commend the
man who contentedly bears old age with poverty more
than the one who does so with wealth?  Indeed, it
is easier not even to recognize what wealth is or
what poverty is.  But many men handle even wealth
along with old age peevishly, and poverty ignobly
and querulously.  And[29] there is no easy way either
for the latter man to handle wealth liberally and
generously[30] or for the former to handle poverty
nobly.  Rather both situations possess the same
character, and whoever can handle much reasonably
can also do the same with the opposite.

          And if it is possible, the poor should remain
in life, but otherwise they should depart readily,
as if from a festival [so also from life].  "Just
as we are ejected from our house," says Bion, "when
the landlord, because he has not received his rent,
takes away the door, takes away the pottery, stops
up the well, in the same way," he says,

16

(16H)  'καὶ ἐκ τοῦ σωματίου ἐξοικίζομαι, / ὅταν ἡ
       μισθώσασα φύσις τοὺς ὀφθαλμοὺς ἀφαιρῆται τὰ
       ὦτα τὰς χεῖρας τοὺς πόδας· οὐχ ὑπομένω, ἀλλ'       155
       ὥσπερ ἐκ συμποσίου ἀπαλλάττομαι οὔθεν δυσχε-
       ραίνων, οὕτω καὶ ἐκ τοῦ βίου· ὅταν [ἢ] ὥρα ᾖ,
       ἔμβα πορθμίδος ἔρυμα.'  ὥσπερ <ὁ> ἀγαθὸς
       ὑποκριτὴς εὖ καὶ τὸν πρόλογον εὖ καὶ τὰ μέσα εὖ
       καὶ τὴν καταστροφήν, οὕτω καὶ ὁ ἀγαθὸς ἀνὴρ        160
       εὖ καὶ τὰ πρῶτα τοῦ βίου εὖ καὶ τὰ μέσα εὖ
       καὶ τὴν τελευτήν· καὶ ὥσπερ ἱμάτιον τρίβωνα
       γενόμενον ἀπεθέμην καὶ οὐ...παρέλκω οὐδὲ
(17H)  φιλοψυχῶ, ἀλλὰ μὴ δυνάμενος ἔτι εὐδαι/μονεῖν
       ἀπαλλάττομαι.                                      165

       Καθάπερ καὶ Σωκράτης· ἦν αὐτῷ ἐκ τοῦ
       δεσμωτηρίου, εἰ ἐβούλετο, ἐξελθεῖν· καὶ τῶν
       δικαστῶν κελευόντων ἀργυρίου τιμήσασθαι οὐ
       προσεῖχεν, ἀλλὰ τῆς ἐν πρυτανείῳ σιτήσεως
       ἐτιμήσατο· καὶ τριῶν ἡμερῶν αὐτῷ δοθεισῶν τῇ       170
       πρώτῃ ἔπιεν καὶ οὐ προσέμεινεν τῆς τρίτης
       ἡμέρας τὴν ἐσχάτην ὥραν παρατηρῶν, εἰ ἔτι ἥλιος
       ἐπὶ τῶν ὁρῶν, ἀλλ' εὐθαρσῶς [τῇ πρώτῃ], <ὡς
       Πλάτων φη>σίν, οὐδὲν τρέψας οὔτε τοῦ προσώπου
       οὔτε τοῦ χρώματος, ἀλλὰ μάλα ἱλαρῶς τε καὶ        175
       εὐκόλως λαβὼν τὸ ποτήριον ἐξέπιεν, καὶ τὸ
       τελευταῖον ἀποκοτταβίσας 'τουτὶ δέ' φησίν
(18H)  ''Ἀλκι/βιάδῃ τῷ καλῷ'' ὅρα σχολὴν καὶ παιδιάν.

       Ἡμεῖς δέ, κἂν ἄλλον <θανατῶντ'> ἴδωμεν,
       πεφρίκαμεν. καὶ μέλλων ἀποθνήσκειν, ἐκάθευδε       180
       βαθέως, ὥστε μόλις διεγεῖραι τινά. ταχύ γ'
       ἂν καὶ ἡμῶν τις ἂν κοιμηθείη....

---

157:  After βίου Hense puts a comma, but a stronger break
      is needed.
163:  See Hense for various attempts to fill the lacuna.
167:  Hense marks an unnecessary lacuna before καί.  See
      note 33.
173:  See note 35.
182:  Hense suggests a lacuna here.  See note 38.

(16H)   "am I being ejected from this poor body when Nature,
the landlady, takes away my eyes, my ears, my hands,
my feet.  I am not remaining, but as if leaving a
banquet and not at all displeased, so also I leave
life: when the hour comes, step on board the
ship.'"[31]  Just as the good actor <performs>[32] well
the prologue, the middle portions and the conclusion, so also does the good man perform well the
first period of life, the middle period, and the
end.  And just as I discarded my cloak when it became threadbare and no..., I do not hold back or
cling fondly to life, but since I can no longer be

(17H)   happy, I am departing.

   So also with Socrates.  It was possible for
him, if he so wished, to leave the prison;[33] and
when the judges proposed that he be fined silver,
he would not pay but instead proposed as a penalty
maintenance in the Prytany.  And although three
days had been allowed him,[34] he drank (the hemlock)
on the first day and did not wait for the last hour
of the third day, watching carefully if the sun was
still upon the mountains, but boldly [on the first
day] <as Plato says> and with no change of expres-
sion or color, but quite cheerfully and contentedly
he took the cup and drained it.[35]  Then dashing out

(18H)   the last drop, he said, "This for beloved Alcibiades."[36]  Observe the seriousness and playfulness.[37]

   And as for us, if we even see another person
<dying>, we shudder.  And on the point of dying, he
fell into such a deep sleep that only with difficulty could anyone arouse him.  And I suppose that
if one of us should fall into that final sleep...[38]

Καὶ γυναικὸς χαλεπότητα πράως ἔφερε
κἀκείνης βοώσης οὐκ ἐφρόντιζεν· ἀλλὰ Κριτοβού-
λου εἰπόντος 'πῶς ἀνέχῃ ταύτης συμβιούσης;'      185
'πῶς δὲ σὺ τῶν παρὰ σοὶ χηνῶν;' 'τί δέ μοι
μέλει ἐκείνων;' φησιν 'οὕτως οὐδ' ἐμοὶ ταύτης,
ἀλλ' ἀκούω ὥσπερ χηνός.' καὶ πάλιν παρειληφό-
τος αὐτοῦ 'Αλκιβιάδην ἐπ' ἄριστον, ὡς ἐκείνη
παρέλθουσα τὴν τράπεζαν ἀνέτρεψεν, οὐκ ἐβόα      190
(19H)   οὐδ' / ὠδύνατο δεινοπαθῶν 'ὦ τῆς παρανομίας,
ὥστε ταύτῃ πάσχειν,' ἀλλ' ἀναλέξας τὰ πέσοντα,
παραθέσθαι πάλιν ἐκέλευσε τὸν 'Αλκιβιάδην· ὡς
δὲ ἐκεῖνος οὐ προσεῖχεν ἀλλ' ἐγκαλυψάμενος
ἐκάθητο [αἰσχυνόμενος], 'προάγωμεν δή' φησιν      195
'ἔξω· φαίνεται γὰρ ἡ Ξανθίππη ὀξυρεγμίᾳ σπα-
ράσσειν ἡμᾶς.'

Εἶτα μετ' ὀλίγας ἡμέρας αὐτὸς ἀριστῶν παρὰ
τῷ 'Αλκιβιάδῃ, ὡς ἡ ὄρνις ἡ γενναία ἐπιπτᾶσα
κατέβαλε τὸν πίνακα, ἐγκαλυψάμενος ἐκάθητο καὶ      200
οὐκ ἤριστα· ὡς δὲ ἐκεῖνος ἐγέλα καὶ ἐπυνθάνετο εἰ διὰ τοῦτο οὐκ ἀριστᾷ ὅτι ἡ ὄρνις ἐπιπτᾶσα καταβάλοι, 'δῆλον ὅτι' φησί 'σὺ μὲν πρῴην
Ξανθίππης ἀνατρεψάσης οὐκ ἐβούλου ἀριστᾶν, ἐμὲ
δὲ οἴει νῦν <ἂν> ἀριστᾶν τῆς ὄρνιθος ἀνατρεψά-      205
σης; ἢ διαφέρειν τι ἐκείνην ὄρνιθος κορυζώσης
ἡγῇ;' 'ἀλλ' εἰ μὲν ὖς' φησίν 'ἀνέτρεψεν, οὐκ
(20H)   ἂν ὠργίζου, [οὐκ ἂν/διηνέχθης] εἰ δὲ γυνὴ ὑώδης;'
ὅρα παιδιάν.

---

199:   For γενναία perhaps γνησία should be read.   See note
       42.

And he bore the crabbiness of his wife with
composure, even when she would scream that he had
no sense. But when Critobulus asked him, "How do
you put up with this woman living with you?" he
replied, "How do you put up with the geese at
your home?" What concern are they to me?" He said,
"In the same way she is no concern to me; rather I
pay as much attention to her as I do to a goose."[39]
And again when he had invited Alcibiades to dinner,[40] she came in and upset the table, but he did
(19H)  not shout or loudly complain in his distress, "Oh,
how indecent that I should have to put up with this
woman!"[41]  Instead, he picked up the fallen objects
and ordered Alcibiades to be served again. But
when his guest paid no attention and sat with his
head covered in shame, Socrates said, "Let's go outside, then, for Xanthippe seems to be causing us in-
digestion."

Then a few days later, he himself was dining at
the home of Alcibiades when a pedigreed bird[42] flew
in and knocked down a platter. Socrates[43] sat with
his head covered in shame and did not eat. When
the other laughed and asked if he was not eating
because the bird had flown in and knocked down the
platter, he replied, "Obviously. The other day,
when Xanthippe did the upsetting you were unwilling
to eat. So do you think that I can eat now when a
bird has done the upsetting? Or do you think that
woman is any different from a drivelling bird?"[44]
"But if," he says,[45] "a sow had done the upsetting,
(20H)  you would not have been angry? [you would not have
been disturbed] Only if a sowish wife did it."
Observe the playfulness.[46]

III

Περὶ φυγῆς

Μήποτε πρὸς μὲν τὸν οἰόμενον ἀλογιστοτέρους τὴν φυγὴν ποιεῖν ὀρθῶς ἂν παραβάλλοιτο τὰ
ἐπὶ τῶν τεχνῶν, ὅτι ὃν τρόπον οὐδὲ αὐλεῖν οὐδὲ
ὑποκρίνεσθαι χεῖρόν ἐστιν ἐπὶ ξένης ὄντα,
οὕτως οὐδὲ βουλεύεσθαι· πρὸς δὲ τὸν κατ' ἄλλο       5
τι ἡγούμενον τὴν φυγὴν βλαβερὸν εἶναι, μὴ οὐδὲν
λέγηται παρὰ τὸ τοῦ Στίλπωνος, ὃ καὶ πρῴην /
(22H)  εἶπον.

'Τί λέγεις,' φησί, 'καὶ τίνων ἡ φυγὴ <ἢ>
ποίων ἀγαθῶν στερίσκει; τῶν περὶ ψυχὴν ἢ τῶν     10
περὶ τὸ σῶμα ἢ τῶν ἐκτός; εὐλογιστίας, ὀρθο-
πραγίας, εὐπραγίας ἡ φυγὴ στερίσκει;

'Οὐ δή.

'Ἀλλὰ μὴ ἀνδρείας ἢ δικαιοσύνης ἢ ἄλλης
τινὸς ἀρετῆς;                                    15

'Οὐδὲ τοῦτο.

'Ἀλλὰ μὴ τῶν περὶ τὸ σῶμά τινος ἀγαθῶν;
ἢ οὐχ ὁμοίως ἔστιν ἐπὶ ξένης ὄντα ὑγιαίνειν καὶ
ἰσχύειν καὶ ὀξὺ ὁρᾶν καὶ ὀξὺ ἀκούειν, ἐνίοτε δὲ
μᾶλλον <ἢ> ἐν τῇ ἰδίᾳ μένοντα;                   20

Καὶ μάλα.

'Ἀλλὰ μὴ τῶν ἐκτὸς στερίσκει ἡ φυγή; ἢ
οὐ πολλοῖς ὤφθη τὰ πράγματα κατὰ τὴν τῶν
τοιούτων ὕπαρξιν ἐπιφανέστερα γεγονότα φυγάδων
γενομένων; ἢ οὐ Φοῖνιξ ἐκ Δολοπίας ἐκπεσὼν ὑπὸ   25
'Ἀμύντορος εἰς Θετταλίαν φεύγει;

        Πηλέα δ' ἐξικόμην,
        καὶ μ' ἀφνειὸν ἔθηκε, πολὺν δέ μοι ὤπασε
                                        λαόν.

---

10:    περὶ <τὴν> ψύχην  Hense, probably incorrectly: cf.
       Diog. Laert. VII. 95.

## III

## On Exile[1]

Perhaps in response to the man who thinks that
exile makes people less competent[2] could aptly be
brought up as a comparison the matter of skills.
Because, just as it is impossible for a man to be a
worse flute-player or actor because he is in a foreign land, so neither is he a worse advisor.[3]  And
to the man who believes that for some other reason
exile is detrimental, let nothing be said contrary
to the writing of Stilpon which I also mentioned
(22H)  the other day:[4]

"What do you mean?" he says, "From what goods
<or> from what sort of goods does exile deprive
one?[5]  Those of the soul or body or of the external
ones?[6]  Prudence, proper conduct, success, does exile deprive you of these?

Of course not!

Well, surely it does not deprive you of courage, righteousness, or any other virtue?

This neither.

Well, surely it does not deprive you of any of
the bodily goods?  Or aren't good health, strength,
keen eyesight and keen hearing the same if a person
is in a foreign land?  Sometimes aren't they even
better <than> if he remains at home?[7]

Very true.

Well, exile does not deprive one of the external goods,[8] does it?  Or don't their affairs,[9] in
so far as the property of such people is concerned,
seem to have become more prominent for many once
they have become exiles?  Or didn't Phoenix, when
he was driven from Dolopia by Amyntor, go into exile in Thessaly?

To Peleus I came,
He made me rich, assigned me many folk.[10]

22

Θεμιστοκλῆς ἐκεῖνος 'ὦ παῖ' φησίν 'ἀπωλόμεθ'  30
(23H)  ἂν εἰ μὴ ἀπωλό/μεθα.'

Νῦν δὲ πολλὴ τῶν τοιούτων ἀφθονία.  ποίων
οὖν ἀγαθῶν ἡ φυγὴ στερίσκει, ἢ τίνος κακοῦ
παραιτία ἐστίν; ἐγὼ μὲν γὰρ οὐχ ὁρῶ.  ἀλλ᾽
ἡμεῖς πολλαχοῦ αὐτοῦς κατορύττομεν καὶ φυγάδες  35
γενόμενοι καὶ ἐν τῇ ἰδίᾳ μένοντες.

Οὐκ ἄρχουσι, φασίν, οὐ πιστεύονται, οὐ
παρρησίαν ἔχουσιν.  ἔνιοι δέ γε καὶ φρουροῦσι
τὰς πόλεις παρὰ βασιλεῦσι, καὶ ἔθνη πιστεύονται, καὶ δωρεὰς μεγάλας καὶ συντάξεις λαμβάν-  40
ουσι.  Λυκῖνος ἐκεῖνος οὐ παρ᾽ ἡμῖν ἐφρούρει
φυγὰς ὢν ἐκ τῆς Ἰταλίας, πιστευόμενος παρ᾽
Ἀντιγόνῳ, καὶ τὸ προστατόμενον ἐποιοῦμεν
Λυκίνῳ ἡμεῖς ἐν τῇ ἰδίᾳ μένοντες; Ἱππομέδων
ὁ Λακεδαιμόνιος ὁ νῦν ἐπὶ Θρᾴκης καθεσταμένος  45
ὑπὸ Πτολεμαίου, Χρεμωνίδης καὶ Γλαύκων οἱ
Ἀθηναῖοι οὐ πάρεδροι καὶ σύμβουλοι, ἵνα μὴ τὰ
παλαιά σοι λέγω, ἀλλὰ τὰ καθ᾽ ἡμᾶς; καὶ τὸ
τελευταῖον οὐκ ἐπὶ στόλου τηλικούτου ἐξαπεστάλη καὶ χρημάτων τοσοῦτον πιστευόμενος καὶ  50
τὴν ἐξουσίαν ἔχων ὡς βούλοιτο χρῆσθαι;

Ἀλλ᾽ ἔν γε τῇ ἰδίᾳ οὐκ ἄρχουσιν οἱ
φυγάδες. /
(24H)  Οὐδὲ γὰρ αἱ γυναῖκες οἴκοι μένουσαι, οὐδ᾽
οἱ παῖδες, οὐδὲ τὰ μειράκια ταυτί, οὐδ᾽ οἱ  55
ἔξωροι τῇ ἡλικίᾳ.  ἀλλὰ μή τι δυσχερὲς αὐτοῖς;
εἰδ᾽ ὠδυνῶντο ἐπὶ τούτῳ, οὐκ ἂν ἦσαν βάκηλοι;
τί δὲ καὶ διαφέρει ἄρχειν καὶ ἰδιωτεύειν; σὺ
πολλῶν [ἢ ὀλίγων] καὶ ἡβώντων βασιλεύεις, ἐγὼ
δὲ ὀλίγων καὶ ἀνήβων παιδαγωγὸς γενόμενος,  60
καὶ τὸ τελευταῖον ἐμαυτοῦ·

---

47: σύμβουλοι; ...ἡμᾶς.  Hense.

And the famous Themistocles says 'Son, we would
(23H)  have been done for if we had not been done in.'"[11]

But nowadays there is a great abundance of
such examples.  Of what sort of goods, then, does
exile deprive, or of what evil is it the cause?
For I certainly don't see.  Indeed, we bury our-
selves in many places and become exiles even while
remaining in our own land.

They (sc. exiles) do not rule, people say;
they are not trusted; they do not have freedom of
speech.  But some do command garrisons in cities
for kings; and they are entrusted with nations, and
they receive great gifts and tributes.  Didn't that
famous Lycinus[12] command a garrison among us when
he was an exile from Italy and was trusted by
Antigonus, and didn't we carry out Lycinus' commands[13] though we remained in our own land?  Doesn't
Hippomedon[14] the Lacedaemonian, now hold an appoint-
ment in Thrace under Ptolemy?  And aren't the Athenians Chremonides and Glaucon assessors and advisers
of Ptolemy,[15] to pass over ancient examples and use
those of our own day?  And finally, wasn't he[16] dis-
patched on such a mission and entrusted with as much
money and with as much authority as he might wish
to use?

But exiles do not rule in their own country.
(24H)  Well, neither do women who stay at home, nor
boys, nor these young men here, nor those who are
past their prime.  But this is not annoying to them,
is it?  And if they were grieved over this, wouldn't
they be effeminate?[17]  Yet what is the difference
between being a ruler and being a private citizen?
You are king over many--and those in the prime of
life; but I over just a few--and they immature boys,
since I am a teacher--, and finally of myself.[18]

τῇ γὰρ αὐτῇ ἐμπειρίᾳ χειρούμενον καὶ τοὺς
πολλοὺς καὶ τὸν ἕνα, καὶ δημοσιεύοντα καὶ
κατ᾽ οἰκίας ἐργολαβοῦντα καὶ ἐπὶ ξένης ὄντα
καὶ ἐν τῇ ἰδίᾳ μένοντα, καὶ κατὰ τὴν αὐτὴν      65
εὐβουλίαν καὶ τῇ ἀρχῇ καλῶς καὶ τῇ ἰδιωτείᾳ
ἔστι χρῆσθαι.  τί οὖν διοίσει μοι, εἰ μὴ ἄρξω
ἀλλὰ ἰδιωτεύσω;

  ᾽Αλλ᾽ οὐδὲ ἐξουσίαν ἕξεις εἰσελθεῖν εἰς
τὴν ἰδίαν.                                       70

  Οὐδὲ γὰρ νῦν εἰς τὸ Θεσμοφόριον ἐξουσίαν
(25Η)  ἔχω, οὐδ᾽ αἱ γυναῖκες εἰς τὸ τοῦ ᾽Ενυαλίου, /
οὐδ᾽ εἰς τὰ ἄβατα ἕξομεν.  ἀλλ᾽ εἰ ἐπὶ τούτῳ
ἄχθοιτό τις, οὐκ ἂν παιδαριώδης εἴη; οὐδὲ εἰς
τὸ γυμνάσιον ἐνίοτε ἐξουσίαν ἔχω, ἀλλ᾽          75
ἀπελθὼν <ἂν> εἰς τὸ βαλανεῖον ἠλειψάμην τῇ
αὐτῇ παλαιστρικῇ χρώμενος ᾗ καὶ πρὸ τοῦ ἐν τῷ
γυμνασίῳ.  οὕτω καὶ δεῦρο ἄβατον ἡγησάμενος
τὴν ἰδίαν μεταβὰς ἀλλαχοῦ κατοικῶ, δύναμαι δὲ
μεταβὰς ὥσπερ ἐξ ἑτέρας νεὼς εἰς ἑτέραν ὁμοίως  80
εὐπλοεῖν, οὕτως ἐξ ἑτέρας πόλεως εἰς ἑτέραν
ὁμοίως εὐδαιμονεῖν.  οὔκουν ἀκλήρημά τι καὶ
ὄνειδος ἐμόν, εἰ μὴ μετὰ πονηρῶν οἰκήσω.  ἢ
ἐμὸν ὄνειδος, ἀλλ᾽ οὐ τῶν ἐμὲ ἐκβαλόντων
ἐπιεικῆ καὶ δίκαιον ὄντα; οὐκ ἀηδῶς Φιλήμων·   85
ἠγωνισμένου γάρ ποτε αὐτοῦ καὶ ἀπηλλαχότος
ἀστείως συναντῶντές τινες 'ὡς εὐημέρηκας'
ἔφασαν 'Φιλῆμον.'  'ὑμεῖς μὲν οὖν' φησιν
'οἴεσθε οὕτω τεθεάμενοι· ἐγὼ μὲν γὰρ ἀεὶ
ἀγαθὸς ὢν διατελῶ.'                             90

---

73:  Hense adopts Wilamowitz's needless deletion of
     ἕξομεν and the addition of οὐθείς.
89:  ἐγὼ μὲν γὰρ  SMA] ἐγὼ δὲ  L, which is better Greek.
     As text stands neither this μὲν nor the one in 88 has
     a corresponding δὲ.

For with the same know-how, whether you manage the
masses or the individual, whether you serve in public or work at home, whether you are in a foreign
land or remain in your own land, it is equally possible with the same good planning to gain advantage
from the political office and from one's private
life.  So what difference will it make to me if I
am not to be a ruler but am to be a private citizen?

But you will not have the right to enter your
own land.

Well, even now I do not have the right to enter the Thesmophorion,[19] nor do women have the right
(25H)  to enter the temple of Enyalius,[20] nor will we have
the right to enter forbidden holy places.  But if
anyone should be upset over this, wouldn't he be
childish?  Sometimes I do not have the right to
go even into the gymnasium, but I have gone off to
the bath and anointed myself with the same wrest-
ling-school stuff[21] which I have used before in the
gymnasium.  In the same way I have hitherto considered my own land impossible to walk upon,[22] and
I have changed residence and now am settling down
elsewhere.  And just as if changing from one ship[23]
to another I can have the same fair sailing, so I
can change from one city to another and have the
same happiness.  At any rate, there is not one bit
of misfortune or disgrace for me, unless I dwell
with wicked men.  Or is the disgrace mine rather
than theirs who expelled me though I was fair and
just?[24]  Not inept was Philemon's remark.  For once
when he had been involved in a legal action and had
gotten off honorably, some men met him and said,
"How lucky you have been, Philemon!"  He replied,
"You feel that way because you have been spectators,
but I think so because I continue to be a good man."

Τί οὖν; ὑπὸ χειρόνων φυγαδεύεσθαι οὐ
παροινία;

Σὺ δ᾽ ἂν ἐβούλου, φησίν, ὑπὸ καλῶν καὶ /
(26H)  ἀγαθῶν; ἢ οὐχ οὕτω μὲν σὸν ἔγκλημα; οὐθένα γὰρ
ἀγνωμόνως καὶ ἀδίκως ἄνδρες ἀγαθοὶ φευγαδεύου-  95
σιν· οὐ γὰρ ἂν ἦσαν δίκαιοι.

Παρευδοκιμεῖσθαι οὖν ὑπὸ τῶν τοιούτων καὶ
χαιροτονίᾳ καὶ ψήφῳ οὐκ ὄνειδος;

Οὐ σόν γε, ἀλλὰ τούτους χειροτονούντων
καὶ ψηφοφορούντων· ὥσπερ εἰ τὸν ἄριστον  100
ἰατρὸν ἀφέντες φαρμακοπώλην εἵλοντο καὶ τούτῳ
τὸ δημόσιον ἔργον ἐνεχείρισαν, πότερον τοῦ
ἰατροῦ εἶπας ἂν ὄνειδος καὶ ἀκλήρημα τοῦτο ἢ
τῶν ἐλομένων;

Ἀλλὰ τοῦτό γε, εὑρεθῆναι τὴν πατρίδα  105
μοχθηρὰν καὶ ἀχάριστον οὖσαν, εἰς ἣν πολλά τις
ἐπόνησε, πῶς οὐκ ἀκλήρημα;

Καὶ πῶς ἂν εἴη τοῦτο ἀκλήρημα, ἀλλ᾽ οὐκ
εἰ δεῖ εἰπεῖν οὕτως εὐκλήρημα τὸ γνῶναι ποία
τις πρότερον μὴ εἰδότα; ἀλλ᾽ εἰ μὲν τὴν  110
γυναῖκα ᾔσθου πονηρὰν καὶ ἐπίβουλον οὖσαν
πρότερον μὴ εἰδώς, ἂν ἔσχες χάριν, καὶ εἰ τὸν
οἰκέτην δραπέτην καὶ κλέπτην, ἵνα φυλάττῃ· εἰ
δὲ τὴν πατρίδα πονηρὰν καὶ ἀχάριστον ᾔσθου,
ἀκληρεῖν ἡγῇ σύ, ἀλλ᾽ οὐ χάριν ἔχεις;  115
(27H)  Ἀλλ᾽ ὅμως μέγα μοι / δοκεῖ τὸ ἐν ᾗ
ἐγένετό τις καὶ ἐτράφη, ἐν ταύτῃ καταγενέσθαι.

What, then?  Isn't it drunken folly to be exiled by inferiors?

(26H)     Would you, he replied,[25] want to be exiled by
good and noble men?[26]  Or isn't this the gist of
your complaint?[27]  For noble men exile no one in a
hard-hearted and unjust manner.  For then they
would not be just.

Then it is no disgrace to be surpassed in the
voting and balloting by such men?

Certainly not yours.  Rather the disgrace be-
longs to those who vote for and elect these men.
It is just as if they dismissed the best physician
and chose a druggist and placed the public task in
his hands.  Would you say that this disgrace and
misfortune belong to the physician or to those who
made the choice?

Well, at any rate, there is this: To have dis-
covered that one's native land, for which he has
labored so much, is knavish and thankless: how is
this not a misfortune?

Nonsense!  How would this be a misfortune?  Indeed, it is not, if one must say that it is good
fortune to have learned someone's character when he
did not know it before.  Yet if you learned that
your wife was wicked and treacherous, though you
did not know it before, you would be gratified. And
if you learned that your servant was a runaway and
a thief, you would be gratified so that you could
take precautions.  Yet, if you have learned that
your native land is wicked and thankless, do you
consider it a misfortune instead of feeling gratitude?[28]

(27H)     But still, it seems a great thing to me to
live in the land where one has been born and bred.[29]

28

Πότερον καὶ ἐν οἰκίᾳ ἐν ᾗ ἐτράφης καὶ
ἐγένου [ἐν ταύτῃ καταγενέσθαι], κἂν ᾖ σαπρὰ
καὶ ῥέουσα καὶ καταπίπτουσα; καὶ ἐν νηῒ ἐν ᾗ          120
ἐγένου καὶ ἐκ παιδίου ἔπλεις, [ἐνταῦσα] κἂν
ἀκάτιον ᾖ, οὐδ' εἰ κωπηλατοῦντα διαρρήγνυσθαι
δέοι, εἰς τὴν εἰκόσορον μεταβάντα ἀσφαλῶς καὶ
ἀκόπως; καὶ ὀνειδίζουσι μὲν ὅτι Κυθήριος, ὅτι
Μυκόνιος, ὅτι Βελβινείτης· ὅμως δὲ μέγα τι          125
φασὶ τὸ ἐν ᾗ ἐγένετό τις καὶ ἐτράφη, ἐν ταύτῃ
καταβιῶναι, καὶ τὰς πλείους μὲν ἐξώλεις τῶν
πόλεων καὶ τοὺς ἐνοικοῦντας ἀσεβεῖς, μέγα δὲ
καὶ προσηνὲς τὴν πατρίδα ὥσπερ καὶ αὐτή.
        Ἀλλὰ καὶ ὅτι μέτοικος ὀνειδίζουσι /          130
(28H)   † δὲ πολλοὶ λέγοντες

                            μέτοικε σύ,
        οὐδε' ἐγγενὴς ὢν τήνδε δουλώσας ἔχεις.

        Καὶ Κάδμον μὲν τὸν κτίστην Θηβῶν θαυμά-
ζεις, ἐμὲ δὲ εἰ μή <εἰμι> πολίτης, ὀνειδίζεις;          135
καὶ Ἡρακλέα μὲν ὡς ἄριστον ἄνδρα γεγονότα
ἐπαινοῦμεν, τὸ δὲ μέτοικον εἶναι ὄνειδος
ἡγούμεθα; Ἡρακλῆς δ' ἐξ Ἄργους ἐκπεσὼν Θήβας
κατῴκει. Λακεδαιμόνιοι οὐδὲν τῶν τοιούτων
ὄνειδος ἡγοῦνται· ἀλλὰ τὸν μὲν μετασχόντα τῆς          140
ἀγωγῆς καὶ ἐμμείναντα, κἂν ξένος κἂν ἐξ εἵλω-
τος, ὁμοίως τοῖς ἀρίστοις τιμῶσι· τὸν δὲ μὴ
ἐμμείναντα, κἂν ἐξ αὐτοῦ τοῦ βασιλέως, εἰς
τοὺς εἵλωτας ἀποστέλλουσι, καὶ τῆς πολιτείας
(29H)   ὁ τοιοῦτος / οὐ μετέχει.          145
        Ἀλλὰ τό γε ἐν τῇ ἰδίᾳ μὴ ἐξεῖναι ταφῆναι
πῶς οὐκ ὄνειδος;

---

119:  This deletion by Wilamowitz may be unnecessary in an
      author as repetitive as Teles.
129:  ὥσπερ καθ' αὐτήν Buecheler, perhaps correctly.

Would you [continue to live] in the house in
which you were bred and born even if it is rotten
and crumbling and falling down?[30]   And would you
remain on a ship[31] on which you were born and sailed
from boyhood, even if it were a little boat, and not,
if you had to burst your gut rowing, change over
willingly and without reluctance to a twenty-oared
ship?[32]   And people use it as a reproach because
someone is from Cythera or Myconos or Belbina.[33]
But still, they say that it is a good thing for
anyone to live out his life in the land in which he
was born and bred, and that, though most of the
cities are pernicious and the inhabitants impious,
one's native land is still a great and comforting
thing just for itself.[34]

(28H)

But many also use it as a reproach that someone is a metic, saying

> You metic,[35]
> Though you're no native, you hold this city
>                                        enslaved.

And you admire Cadmus, the founder of Thebes,
but you reproach me unless <I am> a citizen?  And
we commend Heracles for having become a leading
man, but we consider being a metic a matter of reproach?  Yet Heracles settled down at Thebes after
being exiled from Argos.  The Lacedaemonians consider none of the things like this to be a matter
of reproach.  Instead, the man who has shared their
way of life and has remained true, whether he is a
foreigner or the son of a helot, they honor on a
par with their best men.  But the man who does not
remain true, even if he is the son of the king himself, they relegate to the helots, and such a man
has no share in the state.

(29H)

But not being allowed burial in one's own
land, how is that not a reproach?

Καὶ πῶς μέλλει τοῦτο ὄνειδος εἶναι ὃ τοῖς
ἀρίστοις πολλάκις συνέβη; ἢ τίς τιμὴ αὕτη ἢ
τις τοῖς κακίστοις περιγίνεται; καὶ Σωκράτην    150
μὲν ἐπαινοῦσιν, ὅταν ἐπιλαμβανόμενος ᾿Αθηναίων
λέγῃ· οἱ μὲν γὰρ στρατηγοὶ ἐφ' οἷς καλλωπίζον-
ται, ὑπερόριοι τεθαμμένοι εἰσί, τὰ δὲ ὀνείδη
τῆς δημοκρατίας ἐν τοῖς δημοσίοις τάφοις.
ὅμως δὲ τὸ μὲν ἐπὶ ξένης ταφῆναι ὄνειδος, τὸ    155
δ' ἐν τοῖς δημοσίοις τάφοις τίμιον; τί δὲ
καὶ διαφέρειν ἂν δόξαι ἐπὶ ξένης ταφῆναι
ἢ ἐν τῇ ἰδίᾳ; οὐκ ἀηδῶς γάρ τις τῶν ᾿Αττικῶν
φυγάδων λοιδορουμένου τινὸς αὐτῷ καὶ λέγοντος
'ἀλλ' οὐδὲ ταφήσῃ ἐν τῇ ἰδίᾳ, ἀλλ' ὥσπερ οἱ    160
ἀσεβεῖς ᾿Αθηναίων ἐν τῇ Μεγαρικῇ' 'ὥσπερ μὲν
οὖν' <φησίν> 'οἱ εὐσεβεῖς Μεγαρέων ἐν τῇ
Μεγαρικῇ.' τί γὰρ τὸ διάφορον; 'ἢ οὐ πανταχόθεν,'
(30H)    φησὶν ὁ ᾿Αρίστιππος, 'ἴση καὶ ὅμοια ἡ / εἰς
ᾅδου ὁδός;'    165
    ῍Η τὴν ἀρχὴν εἰ μὴ ταφήσῃ, τί σοι μέλει;
'ἀλλ' ἡ περὶ ταφῆς ἀγωνία,' φησὶν ὁ Βίων, 'πολλὰς
τραγῳδίας ἐποίησεν.' ὥσπερ καὶ ὁ Πολυνείκης
ἐντέλλεται

    θάψον δέ μ' ὦ τεκοῦσα καὶ σὺ σύγγονε    170
    ἐν γῇ πατρῴᾳ, καὶ πόλιν θυμουμένην
    παρηγορεῖτον, ὡς τοσόνδε γοῦν τύχω
    χθονὸς πατρῴας, κεἰ δόμους ἀπώλεσα.

εἰ δὲ μὴ τύχοις χθονὸς πατρῴας, ἀλλ' ἐπὶ
ξένης ταφείς, τί ἔσται τὸ διάφορον; ἢ ἐκ    175
Θηβῶν μὲν εἰς ᾅδου ὁ Χάρων πορθμεύει...;

    καὶ γῆς φίλης ὄχθοισι κρυφθῆναι καλόν. /
(31H)    εἰ δὲ μὴ κρυφθείης, ἀλλὰ ἄταφος <ῥιφθείης>,
    τί τὸ δυσχερές; ἢ τί διαφέρει

---

150: ᾿Ισοκράτην Cobet.
176: Something is clearly missing as Θηβῶν μὲν indicates.

And just how is this going to be a reproach
which often happens to the best men?  Or what honor
is this which is available to the worst men?  Indeed, people commend Socrates when in his attack on
the Athenians[36] he says, "The generals in whom they
pride themselves have been buried outside the bound-
ries of the city, but the disgraces[37] of the republic have been buried in public graves.[38]  Yet burial
in a foreign land is a disgrace, but in public
graves it is an honor?  But what difference would
there seem to be between burial in a foreign land
and in one's own land?  For not inept was the remark of a certain Attic exile.  When someone railed
at him and said, "Why, you won't even be buried in
your own land, but like those Athenians who are impious, you'll be buried in Megarian soil," <he re-
plies>, "Indeed, just like those Megarians who are
pious, in Megarian soil."  For what is the difference?  "Or isn't the road to Hades's realm," asks
(30H)   Aristippus,[39] "equal and alike[40] from any direc-
tion?"

Or, in the first place, what does it matter to
you if you are not to buried?  "Indeed, the anguish
over burial," says Bion, "has composed many trage-
dies."  Just as even Polyneices commands:[41]

> But bury me, Mother and you my sister,
> In my ancestral land, and calm the angry
> City, so that I win at least this much
> Of my ancestral soil, though I've lost home.

But if you should not "win your ancestral soil" but
be buried in a foreign land, what will be the difference?  Or is it from Thebes that Charon ferries
to Hades' realm...[42]

> Tis good to lie beneath a mound of one's
> own land.[43]

(31H)   But if you should not be buried but be tossed
out without a grave,[44] what is so annoying
about that?  Or what is the difference in being

ὑπὸ πυρὸς κατακαυθῆναι ἢ ὑπὸ κυνὸς καταβρωθῆναι 180
ἢ ἐπάνω τῆς γῆς ὄντα ὑπὸ κοράκων ἢ κατορυχθέντα
ὑπὸ σκωλήκων;

συνάρμοσον δέ μου βλέφαρα τῇ σῇ χερί,
μῆτερ.

ἂν δὲ μὴ συναρμόσῃ σου, ἀλλὰ βλέπων καὶ          185
κεχηνὼς ἀποθάνῃς, τί ἔσται τὸ χαλεπόν; ἢ καὶ
τῶν ἐν τῇ θαλάττῃ καὶ ἐν τοῖς πολέμοις ἀπο-
θνησκόντων συναρμόζει τις; ἀλλ' ἔμοιγε δοκεῖ
ταῦτα παιδιά τις ἡμετέρα εἶναι...καὶ ἡμεῖς μὲν
καὶ ἰδεῖν καὶ ἄψασθαι ὀκνοῦμεν·...οἱ δὲ σκε-          190
λετεύσαντες ἔνδον ἔχουσιν ὡς καλόν τι καὶ /
(32H)  ἐνέχυρα τοὺς νεκροὺς λαμβάνουσιν.  οὕτως ἀντ-
έστραπται τῷ ἡμετέρῳ ὁ ἐκείνων τρόπος.

---

190:  More seems to have fallen from the text here.  See
      note 49.

burnt up by fire, eaten up by a dog or being de-
voured by ravens[45] above the ground or by worms
below?[46]

>  And close my eyelids fast with your own hand,
>  Mother.[47]

But should she not "close your eyelids fast," and
you should die stark and staring, what will be the
difficulty?  Or does anyone close the eyes of those
who die at sea or in wars?  But to me at least
these matters seem mere childish play[48]...and we
dread to look at and touch...[49]  But they mummify
(32H)  them and keep them indoors as something good and
accept the bodies as sureties.[50]  Thus their custom
is the opposite of ours.[51]

## IVA

(33H)     Σύγκρασις πενίας καὶ πλούτου

Δοκεῖ μοι ἡ τῶν χρημάτων κτῆσις σπάνεως
καὶ ἐνδείας ἀπολύειν.

Καὶ πῶς; οὐχ ὁρᾷς ἐνίους κεκτημένους μὲν
πόλλα ὡς δοκοῦσιν, οὐ χρωμένους δὲ τούτοις δι'
ἀνελευθερίαν καὶ ῥυπαρίαν; ἀλλ' ὥσπερ ὁ                    5
Πρίαμος οὐδ' ἔτλη ἔξεσθαι ἐπὶ θρόνου /

(34H)     πολλῶν κατὰ οἶκον ἐόντων,

ἀλλὰ χαμαὶ ἐκάθητο

κυλινδόμενος κατὰ κόπρον,

οὕτως ἔνιοι πολλῶν ὑπαρχόντων αὐτοῖς δι'              10
ἀνελευθερίαν οὐδενὸς γεύονται οὐδὲ ἅπτονται·
ἀλλὰ πλείω οἱ μῦς κατεσθίουσι καὶ οἱ μύρμηκες
ἢ αὐτοί. ὥσπερ ὁ Λαέρτης, [ἀγροῦ ἐπ' ἐσχατιῆς
γρηὶ σὺν ἀμφιπόλῳ, ἥ οἱ βρῶσίν τε πόσιν τε
παρτίθει] εἰς ἀγρὸν ἀπελθὼν μόνος μετὰ γραδίου     15
κακουχεῖ αὐτὸν καὶ ξηραίνει, οἱ δὲ μνηστῆρες...
τὰ ἐκείνου. καὶ ὥσπερ ὁ Τάνταλος ἐν λίμνῃ
ἔστηκεν, ὥς φησιν ὁ ποιητής, κατὰ κρατὸς δὲ
καρποί,

ἀλλ' ὁπότ' ἰθύσει' ὁ γέρων                           20

πιεῖν ἢ τῶν καρπῶν ἅψασθαι, ἡ μὲν λίμνη ξηρὰ
ἐγίνετο, /

(35H)     τοὺς δ' ἄνεμος ῥίπτασκε ποτὶ νέφεα σκιόεντα,

οὕτως ἐνίων ἡ ἀνελευθερία καὶ δυσελπιστία καὶ
τὸν οἶνον καὶ τὸν σῖτον καὶ τὴν ὀπώραν ῥίπτασ-      25
κεν, οὐ ποτὶ νέφεα ἀλλ' ἃ μὲν εἰς τὴν ἀγορὰν
ἃ δὲ εἰς τὸ καπηλεῖον, καὶ ἐπιθυμοῦντες οὐδενὸς
γεύονται.

---

16:   Hense is right to think that something is lost here.
      See note 6.
24:   δυσελπιστία] δυσπληστία  Meineke, but see note 8.

IVA

(33H)       A Comparison of Poverty and Wealth[1]

It seems to me that the acquisition of money frees
one from scarcity and want.

And just how?  Don't you see that some men
have acquired large sums, as they think, but do not
use them because of illiberality and meanness?  But
just as Priam did not dare sit upon the throne[2]

(34H)       Though many were throughout the hall

but sat upon the ground[3]

Rolling about in filth[4]

so some men, though they have a great amount, sample none of it because of their illiberality, nor
do they even touch it.  Indeed, mice and ants con-
sume more than they do.  As Laertes [in the out-
skirts of his land with an old servant woman who
served him food and drink][5] goes alone to the country with an old hag and abuses and denies himself,
while the suitors[6]...that famous man's (i.e. Odys-
seus') possessions; and as Tantalus stands in the
pool, as the poet says, and tries with all his
might to pick the fruit,

But whenever the old man tried[7]

to drink or touch the fruit, the pool dried up,

(35H)       And wind would toss the fruit toward shady
clouds.[7]

So, too, the illiberality and despondency[8] of some
men toss wine and food and fruit, not toward the
clouds, but part into the marketplace, part into
the taverns, and though they are full of desire,
they sample nothing.

Καὶ ἐὰν μὲν πρὸς ἕτερον κληθῇ, ἐκπαθῶς
ἀπολαύει, αὐτὸς δὲ ἔχων οὐθενὶ ἂν παρέχοι,                    30
ἀλλ᾽ ἐπιθυμῶν στραγγεύεται· καὶ εἰ μέν τις
αὐτὸν ἐξοικίζοι τὸν τοιοῦτον πολέμιον ἂν ἡγοῖτο,
ἑαυτὸν δὲ ἐξοικίζων οὐ δοκεῖ εἶναι πολέμιος.
οὐκ ἀηδῶς δ᾽ ἔμοιγε δοκοῦσι καὶ οἱ ἀρχαῖοι πρὸς
ταῦτα ἐρωτᾶν· ὃ μὴ ἀπολύει ἀπληστίας καὶ ἀνε-      35
λευθερίας καὶ ἀλαζονείας ἄνθρωπον, οὐδὲ ἐνδείας
οὐδὲ σπάνεως ἀπολύει· οὐθὲν δὲ τῶν τοιούτων
(36H)  ἀπληστίας καὶ ἀνελευ/θερίας καὶ ἀλαζονείας
ἀπολύει· τὸν γὰρ τρόπον οὐ μετατίθησιν· ὥσπερ
οὐδὲ τῶν σωφρονούντων ἡ πενία, ἐὰν ἐκ πλουσίων     40
πένητες γένωνται.  θᾶττον γὰρ ἂν ἔμοιγε δοκεῖ
τις εἰπεῖν ὡς τὴν χρόαν, τὸ μέγεθος, [ἢ] τὴν
ὄψιν μετατίθησιν ἢ τῶν χρημάτων κτῆσις ἥπερ
τὸν τρόπον· ἕως δ᾽ ἂν ᾖ οὗτος ἄπληστος ἀνελεύ-
θερος ἀλαζὼν δειλός, ἐν ἐνδείᾳ καὶ σπάνει         45
ἔσται.

Καὶ πῶς σπανίζουσιν οὗτοι τούτων ἃ ἔχουσι;
Πῶς δὲ οἱ τραπεζῖται, φησὶν ὁ Βίων, χρημάτων, ἔχοντες αὐτά; οὐ γὰρ αὐτῶν ὄντα ἔχουσιν·
οὐδὲ ἄρα οὗτοι αὐτῶν.  εἰ δὲ καὶ τοῦτό τίς σοι      50
δοίη ἐπὶ τοῦ παρόντος, ἀλλ᾽ ὅμοιόν ἐστι τὸ
οὕτως ἔχειν <καὶ τὸ μὴ ἔχειν>, ὅταν ἀδυνατῇς
αὐτοῖς χρῆσθαι.  ἢ τί διαφέρει μὴ ἔχειν ἢ
οὕτως ἔχειν ὡς αἱ Φορκίδες τὸν ὀφθαλμὸν
ἀποκείμεν<ον ἔχειν λέγοντ>αι, αὐτὰς δὲ εἰς        55
φραγμοὺς καὶ βόθρους καὶ βόρβορον ἐμπίπτειν,
μηθὲν προορωμένας, ἀλλ᾽ ἐώσας ἀποκεῖσθαι, ἕως
(37H)  ὅτου καὶ αὐτὸν τὸν ὀφθαλμὸν ὁ Περσεὺς / ὑφείλετο;

---

50:  τοῦτο] ταῦτα should probably be read.  See note 11.
55:  Addition made by Buecheler, but this is probably
     another example of his penchant for tampering with a
     text.

And if the man is invited to another's house for dinner, he enjoys himself passionately. But he himself, though he has the means, shares with no one, but in his greed he holds back.[9] And if someone should eject him from a house, he would consider such a person his enemy; but though he ejects himself, he does not consider himself an enemy. Not ineptly, it seems to me, did even the ancients[10] expound these matters: what does not release a man from insatiability, illiberality and false pretension does not release him from either want or scarcity. None of the things like these frees him from insatiability, illiberality and false pretension, for none of them changes his character. For example, not even poverty changes the character of those who are prudent, if they become poor after being wealthy. For sooner, it seems to me, could one say that the acquisition of money changes skin, size, appearance than it changes character. But as long as this man is insatiable, illiberal, pretentious, worthless, he will live in want and scarcity.

(36H)

And just how are these men deprived of what they have?

Well, how are the bankers, asks Bion, deprived of money while they have it? For they do not really have any of their own, and neither do these men have any of their own. But even if someone should deposit it[11] with you on a temporary basis,[12] such a possession is the same thing <as not having it at all> since you cannot make use of it. Or what difference is there between not having it and having it in the same way as the daughters of Phorcus[13] <are said to> have one eye stored up as a common possession? They stumble into walls, ditches, mudholes, seeing nothing ahead but still leaving it in storage until such time as Perseus steals the eye itself.[14]

(37H)

"Η τί διαφέρει μὴ ἔχειν τροφὴν ἢ τοιαύτην
ἔχειν, ἧς οὐ μὴ γεύσηται· ἰχθῦς καὶ περιστέρια    60
ἢ Αἰγυπτίῳ κύνα ἢ Ἕλληνι κρανίον ἀνθρώπου;
ὁμοίως γὰρ σπανιεῖ τροφῆς καὶ ἔχων ταύτην καὶ
μὴ ἔχων.  τί οὖν ὄφελος τὸ οὕτως ἔχειν; ἐπεὶ
καὶ σὺ ἀργύριον ἔχεις, ἀλλ' οὐ μὴ χρήσῃ διὰ
ῥυπαρίαν καὶ δειλίαν.  διὸ καὶ οἱ ἀρχαῖοι    65
ἔλεγον οὐκ ἀηδῶς· ἔφασαν γὰρ τῶν ἀνθρώπων οὓς
μὲν χρήματα ἔχειν οὓς δὲ κτήματα.  οὓς μὲν γὰρ
χρᾶσθαι τοῖς ὑπάρχουσιν, οὓς δὲ μόνον κεκτῆσθαι
οὔτε ἑαυτοῖς προϊεμένους οὔτε ἄλλοις μεταδιδόν-
(38H)    τας.  καὶ ὃν τρόπον, ὅταν βασιλεὺς ἢ δυνάστης /    70
τὰ ὑπάρχοντα παρασφραγίσηται, οὐκ ἔστιν ἄψασθαι,
οὕτως ἐνίων ἡ ἀνελευθερία καὶ δυσελπιστία τὰ
ὑπάρχοντα παρεσφράγισται οὐκ ἐῶσα ἄψασθαι,
ἀλλὰ σπανίζουσι καὶ ἐν ἐνδείᾳ εἰσίν, ἐπιθυμοῦντες μὲν πολλῶν χρᾶσθαι δὲ οὐ δυνάμενοι.    75

Διὸ καὶ ὁ Κράτης πρὸς τὸν ἐπιζητοῦντα 'τί
οὖν μοι ἔσται φιλοσοφήσαντι;' 'δυνήσῃ' φησί
'τὸ φασκώλιον ῥᾳδίως λῦσαι καὶ τῇ χειρὶ ἐξελὼν
εὐλύτως δοῦναι, καὶ οὐχ ὥσπερ νῦν στρέφων καὶ
μέλλων καὶ τρέμων, ὥσπερ οἱ παραλελυμένοι τὰς    80
χεῖρας· ἀλλὰ καὶ πλῆρες ὂν αὐτὸ οὕτως ὄψει καὶ
κενούμενον ἰδὼν οὐκ ὀδυνήσῃ, καὶ χρᾶσθαι
προελόμενος ῥᾳδίως δυνήσῃ καὶ μὴ ἔχων οὐκ
ἐπιποθήσεις, ἀλλὰ βιώσῃ ἀρκούμενος τοῖς
παροῦσι, τῶν ἀπόντων οὐκ ἐπιθυμῶν, τοῖς    85
(39H)    συμβεβηκόσιν οὐ δυσα/ρεστῶν.'

---

60:    Hense marks a lacuna before ἰχθῦς, but there is no
       real need for it.

Or what difference is there between not having food and having the kind that cannot be tasted: fishes, little doves or for an Egyptian a dog or for a Greek the skull of a man?[15] For the man who has this kind of food and the man who has none are equally deprived of food. What advantage, therefore, is this kind of possession? Though you have money, you still do not make use of it because of sordiness and meanness. Therefore the ancients[16] spoke not ineptly, for they said that some men have cash, some have a cache.[17] For some cash in on their resources, but some only cache them away without spending them on themselves or sharing with (38H) others. And just as when a king or ruler sets a upon his resources, it is impossible to touch them, so some men's illiberality and despondency[18] set a seal upon their resources, not allowing them to touch them. Instead, they deprive themselves and are in want, still desiring large sums but unable to cash in on them.

And therefore Crates replied to the man who asked, "What will be in it for me after I have become a philosopher?" "You will be able," he said, "to open your wallet easily and with your hand scoop out and dispense lavishly instead of, as you now do, squirming and hesitating and trembling like those with paralyzed hands. Rather, if the wallet is full, that is how you will view it; and if you see that it is empty, you will not be distressed. And once you have elected to use the money, you will easily be able to do so; and if you have none, you will not yearn for it, but you will live satisfied with what you have, not desiring what you do not have nor displeased with whatever comes your (39H) way."

Καὶ εἴ τις βούλεται ἢ αὐτὸς ἐνδείας καὶ
σπάνεως ἀπολυθῆναι ἢ ἄλλον ἀπολῦσαι, μὴ χρήματα
αὐτῷ ζητείτω. ὅμοιον γάρ, φησὶν ὁ Βίων, ὡς εἴ
τις τὸν ὑδρωπικὸν βουλόμενος παῦσαι τοῦ δίψους,      90
τὸν μὲν ὕδρωπα μὴ θεραπεύοι, κρήνας δὲ καὶ
ποταμοὺς αὐτῷ παρασκευάζοι. ἐκεῖνος τε γὰρ
ἂν πρότερον πίνων διαρραγείη ἢ παύσαιτο τοῦ
δίψους, οὗτός τε οὐκ ἄν ποθ᾽ ἱκανωθείη, ὅταν
ᾖ ἄπληστος καὶ δοξοκόπος καὶ δεισιδαίμων.           95
διὸ καὶ εἰ βούλει τὸν υἱόν σου τῆς ἐνδείας
(40H)    καὶ σπάνεως παῦσαι, μὴ πρὸς τὸν Πτολεμαῖον /
πέμπε ὅπως χρήματα κτήσεται· εἰ δὲ μή, ἀλαζο-
νείαν προσλαβὼν ἀπελεύσεται, περανεῖς δὲ οὐδέν·
ἀλλὰ [εἰς ἀκαδημίαν] πρὸς Κράτητα· ἐκεῖνος      100
ἠδύνατο ἐξ ἀπλήστων καὶ πολυτελῶν ἐλευθερίους
καὶ ἀφελεῖς κατασκευάζειν.

Καὶ Μητροκλῆς δὲ ἐκεῖνος ἔφη, ὡς ἔοικεν,
ὅτε μὲν παρὰ Θεοφράστῳ καὶ Ξενοκράτει σχολάζοι,
πολλῶν αὐτῷ ἐξ οἴκου ἀποστελλομένων φοβεῖσθαι      105
μὴ τῷ λιμῷ ἀποθάνοι καὶ ἀεὶ σπανίζειν καὶ
ἐνδεὴς εἶναι, μεταβὰς δὲ ὕστερον πρὸς Κράτητα
κἂν ἄλλον προστρέφειν οὐδενὸς πεμπομένου.
τότε μὲν γὰρ ἐξ ἀνάγκης ἔδει ὑπόδημα ἔχειν,
καὶ τοῦτο ἀκάττυτον [ἥλους οὐκ ἔχον], εἶτα      110
χλανίδα, παίδων ἀκολουθίαν, οἰκίαν μεγάλην,
εἰς τὸ σύνδειπνον ὅπως ἄρτοι καθαροί, ὄψον
(41H)    μὴ τὸ τυχόν, οἶνος ἡδύς, ὑποδοχὰς / τὰς ἐπι-
βαλλούσας, ἵνα πολυτελῶς· ἐλευθέριος γὰρ παρ᾽
αὐτοῖς ἡ τοιαύτη ἀναστροφὴ ἐκρίνετο· πρὸς      115
Κρήτητα δὲ μεταβάντι οὐδὲν ἦν τούτων· ἀλλ᾽
ἀφελέστερος τῷ τρόπῳ γενόμενος ἠρκεῖτο τρίβωνι
καὶ μάζῃ καὶ λαχανίοις οὐκ ἐπιποθῶν τὴν προτέραν
δίαιταν οὐδὲ τῇ παρούσῃ δυσχεραίνων.

---

89:    αὑτῷ Blass, printed by Hense] αὐτῷ MSS.   See note 19.

And if anyone wants either to have himself
freed from want and scarcity or to free someone
else, let him not seek money for him.[19] For it is,
says Bion, as if someone who wants to relieve the
thirst[20] of a man suffering from dropsy would not
treat the dropsy but would supply him with springs
and rivers. For the sufferer would sooner burst
with drinking than be cured of thirst. And this
man[21] could never be satisfied, since he is insatiable, thirsting for fame and superstitious.[22]
Therefore if you want your son to be freed from

(40H) want and scarcity, do not send him to Ptolemy to
get money. Otherwise he will return after acquir-
ing pretension as well, and you will accomplish
nothing. But go [to the Academy and][23] to Crates:
he could change men from insatiable and extravagant
to liberal and unpretentious.

Even the famous Metrocles[24] said, as it seems,
that when he was studying with Theophrastus and
Xenocrates, although many things were being sent to
him from home, he was in constant fear of dying from
hunger and was always destitute and in want. But
when he later changed over to Crates, he could feed
even another person though nothing was sent from
home.[25] For in the former case, of necessity he
had to have shoes, and these without stitches
[without nails], then a cloak, a retinue of servants,
a large house; for the common table he had to see
that the breads were good, the dainties above the

(41H) ordinary, the wine sweet, the entertainment appropriate; think how expensive that is![27] For such a
way of life is considered among them to be gen-
teel.[28] But when he went to Crates, there was none
of these things. Instead he became less pretentious
in his habits and was satisfied with a threadbare
cloak, barley-cake and green vegetables, no longer
desiring his previous way of life nor distressed at
his present lot.

42

Πρὸς ῥῖγος ἡμεῖς μὲν ζητοῦμεν παχύτερον    120
ἱμάτιον, ἐκεῖνος δὲ διπλώσας τὸν τρίβωνα
περιῄει τρόπον τινὰ δύο ἱμάτια ἔχων.  εἰ
ἀλείψασθαι χρείαν ἔχοι, εἰσελθὼν ἂν εἰς τὸ
βαλανεῖον τῷ γλοιῷ ἠλείψατο.  καὶ βαδίσας
ἐνίοτε πρὸς τὴν κάμινον οὖ τὰ χαλκεῖα, τῶν    125
μανίδων ἀπόπυριν ποιήσας, περιχέας ἂν ἐλάδιον
καθίσας ἠρίστησε.  καὶ ἐκάθευδε τὸ μὲν θέρος
ἐν τοῖς ἱεροῖς, τὸν δὲ χειμῶνα ἐν τοῖς βαλανεί-
οις· οὐ σπανίζων ὥσπερ πρὸ τοῦ οὐδὲ ἐνδεὴς ὤν,
ἀλλ' ἀρκούμενος τοῖς παροῦσι, διακόνους οὐκ    130
ἐπιθυμῶν ἔχειν.  θαυμαστὸν μὲν γάρ, φησὶν <ὁ
Διογένης>, εἰ Μάνης μὲν Διογένους ἄνευ δυνήσεται ζῆν, Διογένης δὲ ἄνευ Μάνους οὐ δυνήσεται
θαρρεῖν.

(42H)
Ὅταν δὲ ποιήσας ἀλαζόνα πολυτελῆ δεισι-    135
δαίμονα δο/ζοκόπον ἄπληστον χρήματα πολλὰ
διδῷς, οὐδὲν περανεῖς.  οὐκ ἀηδῶς γὰρ ὁ
Φιλήμων

πλοῦτον μεταλήψεσθ' ἕτερον, οὐχ ἕστερον
τρόπον.    140

ποὑτου δὲ μένοντος τοῦ αὐτοῦ ὁμοίως οὐκ ἀρκεῖ-
ται οὐδ' ἱκανοῦται, ἀλλ' ἐπιθυμίας καὶ ἐπιβολὰς
τοσούτων καὶ τοιούτων ἔχει, ἐξ ὧν ἐν ἐνδείᾳ καὶ
σπάνει ἔσται·

ἄπληστον γὰρ ἔχουσι κακοὶ νόον.    145

Καὶ παῖς μὲν ὢν ἐπιθυμεῖ ἔφηβος γενέσθαι,
ἔφηβος δὲ γενόμενος ζητεῖ πάλιν τὸ χλαμύδιον
ἀποθέσθαι, ὅταν δὲ ἀνδρωθῇ πάλιν εἰς τὸ γῆρας
σπεύδει.  νῦν δέ, φησίν, ἀβίωτος ὁ βίος,
στρατεία, λειτουργία, πολιτικὰ πράγματα,    150
σχολάσαι [αὐτῷ] οὐκ ἔστι.  πρεσβύτης γέγονε·
πάλιν ἐπιθυμεῖ τὰ ἐν νεότητι,

---

131:  Added by Hense, following Meineke.  Is it necessary?
      The subject of φησὶν can be Metrocles, who is quoting
      words of Diogenes which by now had become almost a
      Cynic proverb.
149:  Perhaps νῦν δὲ γάρ should be read.  See note 37.

Against the cold we look for a thicker garment, but he used to double the threadbare cloak
and go around as if wearing two.[29] If he needed
to be anointed, he would go into the bath and
anoint himself with second-hand scrapings.[30] And
he would occasionally go to the furnace in the
bronze-foundry, fry some sprats, douse them with a
little oil,[31] sit down and make a meal. And in
summer he would sleep in sanctuaries, in winter in
the baths,[32] no longer destitute as he had been before nor in want. Instead he was satisfied with
his present lot and did not feel the desire to have
servants. "For it is remarkable," says <Diogenes>,
"if Manes[33] can live without Diogenes, but Diogenes
cannot fare well without Manes."

(42H) But once you have made yourself pretentious,
extravagant, superstitious, athirst for fame, insatiable, even if you spend a lot of money, you will
accomplish nothing. For not ineptly did Philemon
say[34]

Another fortune you'll acquire, not another
character.

And as long as this man remains the same, he will
be neither content nor satisfied. Instead he will
retain his desires and appetites for things of this
magnitude and type. Consequently, he will live in
scarcity and want.

For the wicked have an insatiable mind[35]

And being a child[36] he longs to become a youth;
and once he's become a youth, again he looks forward to putting aside the cloak of youth; and when
he reaches his prime, again he is eager for old
age. But now,[37] says he, life is unlivable:[38] cam-
paigning, public duties, political affairs--it's
impossible to enjoy any leisure. He's an old man:
again he longs for the things of childhood,

ἡ νεότης μοι φίλον ἀεί, τὸ δὲ γῆρας
βαρύτερον Αἴτνης, /

(43H)  καὶ μακαρίζει τὸν τοῦ παιδὸς βίον.               155

Οἰκέτης ἐστίν· ἐλεύθερος σπεύδει γενέσθαι·
κἂν τούτου τύχω, φησί, πάντ' ἔχω. γέγονεν
ἐλεύθερος· δοῦλον εὐθὺς ἐπιθυμεῖ κτήσασθαι.
γέγονε τοῦτ' αὐτῷ· ἕτερον πρὸς σπεύδει κτήσα-
σθαι· μία γάρ, φησί, χελιδὼν ἔαρ οὐ ποιεῖ.        160
εἶτα δόμον, εἶτα κάγρόν, εἶτ' Ἀθηναῖος γενέσθαι, εἶτα ἄρξαι, εἶτα βασιλεῦσαι, εἶτα, ὥσπερ
Ἀλέξανδρος, ἀθάνατος γενέσθαι· εἰ δὲ καὶ τούτου τύχοι, οἶμαι, ἵνα Ζεὺς γένηται ἐπιθυμήσει.

Πῶς οὖν ὁ τοιοῦτος οὐκ ἐνδεής; ἢ ποία        165
χρημάτων ὕπαρξις <τῶν> τοιούτων ἐπιθυμιῶν
ἀπολύει; οἱ βασιλεῖς αὐτοὶ πολλῆς ἐπάρχοντες
καὶ προσόδους μεγάλας ἔχοντες οὐδὲν ἧττον
σπανίζουσιν, ὥστε καὶ τυμβωρυχεῖν καὶ ἱεροσυ-
λεῖν καὶ παρὰ τὸ προσῆκον φυγαδεύειν. ἅμα       170
γὰρ τῇ ἀρχῇ πολλὰ τὰ ἀναγκαῖα ἀναπεπλάκασι,
καὶ οὔτε τῆς ἀρχῆς ἀποστῆναι προαιροῦνται οὔτε
τὰ καθ' ἑαυτοὺς λιτότερον διεξάγουσιν· εἶτα
ἀναγκάζονται πολλὰ ὧν <οὐ> βούλονται.

(44H)     Εἰ δὲ πάντων τις / τῶν τοιούτων ὑπεράνω    175
γένοιτο, ἐν πολλῇ ἂν εἴη ἀνδείᾳ καὶ ἀσπανισ-
τίᾳ. οὐκ ἀηδῶς γὰρ Κράτης

οὐκ οἶσθα,

φησί,

πήρα δύναμιν ἡλίκην ἔχει,               180
θέρμων τε χοῖνιξ καὶ τὸ μηδενὸς μέλειν.

---

159:  πρὸς σπεύδει Meineke] προσσπεύδει MSS.  Both read-
      ings are awkward.
161:  δόμον Jacobs] δύο MSS and defended by Hense.  Hense
      also marks an unnecessary lacuna after Ἀθηναῖος.
181:  μέλειν Diogenes Laertius VI. 86] μέλλειν MSS.
      μέλειν is obviously correct: 1) The meter excludes
      μέλλειν; 2) Teles' words in 183-84 paraphrase τὸ
      μηδενὸς μέλειν.

My youth was ever dear to me, but old age is
more burdensome than Aetna.[39]

(43H)   And he deems a child's life fortunate.

He's a slave. He's eager to be free and says,
"If I get this, I have everything." He becomes
free: immediately he longs to acquire a slave. He
get's one: he's eager to acquire a second as well,
"for one swallow does not make a spring."[40] Then
he's eager to acquire[41] a house,[42] a plot of land,
then to become an Athenian, then to be a magistrate,
then a king, then, like Alexander, to become immortal. And if he should achieve this, I suppose he
would yearn to become Zeus.

How, then, is such a person not in want? Or
what amount of money removes such desires? Kings
themselves, though they rule over a large domain
and possess great revenues, are nonetheless destitute. Consequently, they break into tombs, rob
graves, and cause banishments[43] in an unseemly
fashion. For along with their reign they vainly
imagine that their necessities are many, but it is
not their policy to step down from the rule, nor do
they manager their affairs more frugally. They
then are compelled to do many things which they <do
not> want to do.

(44H)   But if anyone could rise above all such
things, he would be in the midst of plenty and
superabundance.[44] For not ineptly did Crates say:

You know not how much power a wallet has,
A peck of lupines and concern for nothing.[45]

τῷ ὄντι μέγα καὶ ἀξιόλογον καὶ πήρας καὶ
θέρμων καὶ λαχάνων καὶ ὕδατος <τὸ> μηδενὸς
φροντίζειν, ἀλλ' εἶναι ἀθώπευτον καὶ ἀκολα-
κευτον.                                                    185

Actually, it is a great and noteworthy thing to
take no heed even of a wallet, lupines, vegetables,
water, but rather to be unkempt and uncompromis-
ing.[46]

48

(45H)　　　Ἡ πενία κωλύει πρὸς τὸ φιλοσοφεῖν, ὁ δὲ
πλοῦτος εἰς ταῦτα χρήσιμον.

　　　Οὐκ εὖ.　πόσους γὰρ οἴει δι' εὐπορίαν ἢ
δι' ἔνδειαν κωλυθῆναι σχολάζειν; ἢ οὐχ ὁρᾷς
ὅτι ὡς ἐπὶ τὸ πολὺ οἱ πτωχότατοι φιλοσοφοῦσιν,　　5
οἱ δὲ πλούσιοι διὰ ταῦτ' αὐτὰ ἐν τῇ πάσῃ
ἀσχολίᾳ εἰσίν; οὐ καλῶς δὲ καὶ Θέογνις λέγει

　　　πολλῷ τοι πλείους λιμοῦ κόρος ὤλεσεν
　　　　　　　ἄνδρας.

ἐπεὶ ποῦ ἂν δείξειας δι' ἔνδειαν κεκωλυμένους　　10
φιλοσοφεῖν, ὥσπερ διὰ πλοῦτον; ἢ οὐχ ὁρᾷς ὅτι
(46H)　δια μὲν ἔνδειαν καρτερεῖν βιάζονται, / διὰ δὲ
πλοῦτον τὰ ἐναντία; ὅταν γάρ, οἶμαι, τῷ
ἀνθρώπῳ προσγένηται εὐκαίρως πορίζεσθαι ὧν ἂν
ἐπιθυμῇ, οὐκέτι οὗτος πρὸς τὸ πονεῖν ἢ ζητεῖν　　15
τι ἐστίν, ἀλλ' ἔχων συνεργὸν τὸν πλοῦτον τῇ
αὐτοῦ κακίᾳ, οὐδεμιᾶς ἡδονῆς ἀπέχεται.　ἢ πάλιν
οὐχ ὁρᾷς διότι οἱ μὲν πλούσιοι πλείω πράττοντες κωλύονται τοῦ σχολάζειν, ὁ δὲ πένης οὐκ
ἔχων τί πράττῃ, πρὸς τὸ φιλοσοφεῖν γίνεται;　　20
Ζήνων ἔφη Κράτητα ἀναγινώσκειν ἐν σκυτείῳ
καθήμενον τὸν Ἀριστοτέλους Προτρεπτικόν, ὃν
ἔγραψε πρὸς Θεμίσωνα τὸν Κυπρίων βασιλέα λέγων
ὅτι οὐδενὶ πλείω ἀγαθὰ ὑπάρχει πρὸς τὸ φιλο-
σοφῆσαι· πλοῦτόν τε γὰρ πλεῖστον αὐτὸν ἔχειν　　25
ὥστε δαπανᾶν εἰς ταῦτα, ἔτι δὲ δόξαν ὑπάρχειν
αὐτῷ.　ἀναγινώσκοντος δὲ αὐτοῦ τὸν σκυτέα ἔφη
προσέχειν ἅμα ῥάπτοντα,

---

1:　πρὸς　MSS] πως　Nauck.　See note 2.
14:　εὐκαίρως Gesner] εὐχερῶς MSS; εὐχαίρως Trincavelli.
　　　See note 5.

$$IVB^1$$

(45H)  Poverty is a deterrent to being a philosopher,[2]
But wealth is a useful thing for this.

Not well spoken. For how many men do you
think have been kept from inactivity[3] because of
wealth rather than because of want? Or don't you
see that, in general, the poorest men are philosophers, but the wealthy are involved in every activity[3] because of these very possessions? Not
badly, then, does Theognis say[4]

> Repletion has destroyed more men by far
> than hunger.

For how could you demonstrate that men are kept
from being philosophers because of want as they are
(46H)  because of wealth? Or don't you see that because
of poverty they are compelled to endure patiently,
but because of wealth there is the reverse situation? For in my opinion, whenever a man happens
to be easily[5] provided with whatever he desires,
he is no longer interested in working[6] or making
any philosophical investigation,[7] but with wealth
as co-worker in his wickedness, he refrains from
no pleasure. Or again, don't you see that the
rich are barred from inactivity because they are
doing more, but the poor man, not knowing what he
should do,[8] devotes himself to being a philosopher?[9]
Zeno said that Crates was sitting in a shoemaker's
shop[10] and reading aloud Aristotle's *Protrepticus*[11]
which he had written for Themison, the Cyprian king.
In it he said that no one had more advantages for
being a philosopher, for he had great wealth so
that he could spend money on this activity and
still have his standing[12] intact. And Zeno said
that while Crates was reading, the shoemaker was
attentive but all the while kept on with his

καὶ τὸν Κράτητα εἰπεῖν 'ἐγώ μοι δοκῶ, ὦ Φιλίσκε,
γράφειν πρὸς σὲ προτρεπτικόν· πλείω γὰρ ὁρῶ          30
σοι ὑπάρχοντα πρὸς τὸ φιλοσοφῆσαι <ἢ> ᾧ ἔγραψεν
Ἀριστοτέλης.'

    Ἢ πάλιν οἰκέται μὲν οἱ τυχόντες αὐτοὺς
(47H)  τρέφουσι καὶ μισθὸν τελοῦσι / τοῖς κυρίοις,
ἐλεύθερος δὲ ἀνὴρ αὐτὸν τρέφειν οὐ δυνήσεται;          35
ἐπεὶ καὶ τῶν τοιούτων φροντίδων μοι δοκεῖ ὁ
ἄβιος λελυμένος πολὺ εὐσχολώτερος εἶναι τῷ
μηδὲν ὑπάρχειν.  οἷον δήπου ἐν τῷ νῦν πολέμῳ
περὶ οὐδενὸς φροντίζει ἢ περὶ αὐτοῦ, ὁ δὲ
πλούσιος καὶ περὶ ἑτέρων.  οὐ κακῶς οὖν οὐδὲ          40
Σοφοκλῆς πεποίηκε λέγοντα τὸν Οἰδίπουν

    τὸν μὲν γὰρ ὑμῶν ἄλγος εἰς ἕν' ἔρχεται,
    ἐγὼ δ' ἐμαυτὸν καὶ πόλιν καὶ σὲ στένω.

ἀλλ' ὅμως ταῦθ' ὁρῶντες γινόμενα οὐδὲν ἧττον
κακοδαιμονεῖν οἴονται, κἂν πένητες ὦσι.·          45

    Φασὶ δὲ καὶ ἐν ταῖς πόλεσιν ἐντιμοτέρους
εἶναι μᾶλλον τοὺς πλουσίους τῶν πενήτων.  οἱ
τοιοῦτοι δέ μοι δοκοῦσιν οὐκ ἀκούειν διότι
(48H)  Ἀριστείδης πτωχότατος ὢν πάντων / Ἀθηναίων
ἐντιμότατος ἦν, καὶ ὅτε τοὺς φόρους ταῖς          50
πόλεσιν ἤθελον τάξαι Ἀθηναῖοι, ἐκεῖνον κατέ-
στησαν, οὐδένα οἰόμενοι δικαιότερ' ἂν τάξαι·
καὶ ὅτι Καλλίας πλουσιώτατος ὢν Ἀθηναίων μᾶλλον
προσεποιεῖτο Ἀριστείδου οἰκεῖος εἶναι ἢ Ἀριστείδης Καλλίου, καὶ πολὺ μᾶλλον ᾐσχύνετο Ἀρισ-          55
τείδης ἐπὶ τῷ πλούτῳ <τῷ> Καλλίου, ἢ Καλλίας
ἐπὶ τῇ πενίᾳ τῇ Ἀριστείδου.

    Ἢ πάλιν Λυσάνδρου τοῦ Σπαρτιάτου τίς
ἐντιμότερος γέγονεν ἢ τιμῶν πλειόνων ἠξιώθη;
καὶ οὗτος τὰς θυγατέρας οὐκ ἐδύνατο ἐκδόσθαι          60
προῖκα δούς.

stitching. And Crates said, "Philiscus, I think
that I should write you an exhortation (*protrepticus*), for I see that you have more advantages for
being a philosopher than the man for whom Aristotle
wrote."

(47H)     Or again, don't ordinary household slaves support themselves and pay a fee to their master,
while the free man will be unable to support himself? Therefore, it seems to me that the unem-
ployed man, freed from such cares, enjoys his inactivity more[13] because he has nothing. For example,
in the present[14] war he is concerned about nothing
but himself, but the rich man is concerned about
others as well. Not badly, therefore, has Sophocles
portrayed Oedipus saying[15]

> For your anguish goes out to one,
> But I groan for myself, the state and you.

But yet, when they see these things happening, they
still consider themselves unhappy, even if they are
poor.

    And they also say that in the cities the rich
are more honored than the poor. Such people seem
to me not to have heard that Aristeides, the poor-
(48H) est of all the Athenians, was most honored and that
when the Athenians wanted to impose taxes on the
states, they appointed him, thinking that no one
would tax more justly, and that Callias, the rich-
est of the Athenians, was appointed to be Aristeides' clerk rather than Aristeides the clerk of
Callias. And much more was Aristeides embarrassed
by the wealth of Callias than Callias was by the
poverty of Aristeides.[16]

    Or again, who became more honored than the
Spartan Lysander or who was deemed worthy of more
honors? And yet this man could not provide a dowry

<καὶ> ἄλλους δὲ ὁπόσους θέλεις ἄν τις εἴποι,
οἳ πένητες ὄντες ἐν μείζονι τιμῇ ἐγένοντο τῶν
πλουσίων.   οὐκ ἀπὸ τρόπου δέ μοι δοκεῖ οὐδ᾿
ὁ Εὐριπίδης ἐγκωμιάζων λέγειν τὸν Ἐτεοκλέα      65
διότι νεανίας μὲν ἐνδεὴς ἦν,

      πλείστας δὲ τιμὰς ἔσχ᾿ ἐν Ἀργείων πόλει.

and marry off his daughters.[17]  <And> one could
also name as many others as you could want who,
though poor, were held in greater honor than the
rich.  Not unreasonably, I think, does Euripides
say in praise of Eteocles[18] that he was a poor
young man

   But was most honored in the Argives' town.

54

V

Περὶ τοῦ μὴ εἶναι τέλος ἡδονήν

Εἰ δὲ δεῖ τὸν εὐδαίμονα βίον ἐκ τῶν
πλεοναζουσῶν ἡδονῶν συγκρῖναι, οὐδείς, φησὶν
ὁ Κράτης, εὐδαίμων γεγονὼς ἂν εἴη. ἀλλ' εἰ
θέλει τις ἐκλογίσασθαι ἐν ὅλῳ τῷ βίῳ πάσας
τὰς ἡλικίας, εὑρήσει πολλῷ πλείους τὰς ἀλγη-          5
δόνας.

Πρῶτον μὲν γὰρ τοῦ πάντος χρόνου ὁ ἥμισυς
ἀδιάφορος, ἐν ᾧ καθεύδω. εἶθ' ὁ πρῶτος ὁ κατὰ /
(50H) τὴν παιδοτροφίαν ἐπίπονος. πεινᾷ τὸ παιδίον,
ἡ δὲ τροφὸς κατακομίζει· διψᾷ, ἡ δὲ λούει·          10
κοιμηθῆναι θέλει, ἡ δὲ κρόταλον ἔχουσα ψοφεῖ.

Εἰ δ' ἐκπέφευγε τὴν τιτθήν, παρέλαβε πάλιν
ὁ παιδαγωγός, παιδοτρίβης, γραμματοδιδάσκαλος,
ἀρμονικός, ζωγράφος. προάγει ἡλικία· προσγίνε-
ται ἀριθμητικός, γεωμέτρης, πωλοδάμνης, [ὑπὸ          15
τούτων πάντων μαστιγοῦται]· ὄρθρου ἐγείρεται·
σχολάσαι οὐκ ἔστιν.

Ἔφηβος γέγονεν· ἔμπαλιν τὸν κοσμητὴν
φοβεῖται, τὸν παιδοτρίβην, τὸν ὁπλομάχον, τὸν
γυμνασίαρχον. ὑπὸ πάντων τούτων μαστιγοῦται,          20
παρατηρεῖται, τραχηλίζεται.

Ἐξ ἐφήβων ἐστὶ καὶ ἤδη εἴκοσι ἐτῶν· ἔτι
φοβεῖται καὶ παρτηρεῖ καὶ γυμνασίαρχον καὶ
στρατηγόν. παρακοιτεῖν εἴ που δεῖ, οὗτοι παρα-
κοιτοῦσι· φυλάττειν καὶ ἀγρυπνεῖν, οὗτοι φυλάτ-
τουσιν· εἰς τὰ πλοῖα ἐμβαίνειν, οὗτοι ἐμβαίν-
ουσιν.

Ἀνὴρ γέγονε καὶ ἀκμάζει· στρατεύεται
καὶ πρεσβεύει ὑπὲρ τῆς πόλεως,

V

(49H)　　　On Pleasure Not Being the Goal of Life

If it is necessary to measure the happy life
from an excess of pleasure, no one, says Crates,
can really be happy.  Indeed, if anyone wants to
add up all the stages in his whole life, he will
find that troubles are far more numerous.[1]

For first, half of all the time, in which I
(50H)　sleep, goes for naught.[2]  Then, the first stage,
that spent being reared as a child, is troublesome.
The child is hungry, but the nurse tries to lull
him to sleep.  He's thirsty, but she gives him a
bath.  He wants to sleep, she makes a racket with a
rattle.

If he escapes the nurse, there to grab him in
turn are the tutor, the physical education teacher,
the grammar teacher, the music teacher, the painter.
The stage advances: Here comes the teacher of math-
ematics, of geometry, the horse trainer.  [By all
of these he is beaten.]  He is awakened at dawn;
it's impossible to get a minute's leisure.

Now he is a youth: Again he fears the magistrate in charge of youths, the physical education
teacher, the teacher of weaponry, the master of the
gymnasium.  By all these he is beaten, closely
supervised, dragged around by his neck.

He's out of his youth and now is twenty years
old: Still he fears and watches closely both the
master of the gymnasium and the general.  There is
need to keep watch somewhere, these youths keep
watch; a need to stand guard and lose sleep, these
stand guard; a need to embark on ships, these embark.

He's become a man and is in his prime: he
serves in the army, goes on embassies for the state,

πολιτεύεται, στρατηγεῖ, χορηγεῖ, ἀγωνοθετεῖ·     30
μακαρίζει ἐκεῖνον τὸν βίον, ὃν παῖς ὢν ἐβίωσε.

    Παρήκμασε καὶ ἔρχεται εἰς γῆρας· πάλιν
παιδοτροφίαν ὑπομένει καὶ ἐπιποθεῖ τὴν νεότητα.
καὶ /

(51Η)      ἡ νεότης μοι φίλον, τὸ δὲ γῆρας     35
           βαρύτερον Αἴτνης.

οὐχ ὁρῶ οὖν, πῶς εὐδαίμονά τις βίον ἔσται
βεβιωκώς, εἴπερ δεῖ τῷ πλεονασμῷ τῶν ἡδονῶν
ἐκμετρῆσαι.

serves as a politician, as general, pays for a
dramatic chorus, presides at games.  He considers
the life he lived as a boy to be happy.

He's past his prime and approaching old age:
again he submits to being waited on like a child
and longs for his youth and (exclaims)

(51H)       My youth was dear to me, but old age is
            more burdensome than Aetna.[3]

I do not see how anyone will live a happy life if
he really must measure it by an excess of pleasure.

## VI

Περὶ περιστάσεων

    Ἡ τύχη ὥσπερ ποιήτριά τις οὖσα παντοδαπὰ
ποιεῖ πρόσωπα, ναυαγοῦ, πτωχοῦ, φυγάδος, ἐν-
δόξου, ἀδόξου. δεῖ οὖν τὸν ἀγαθὸν ἄνδρα πᾶν
ὅ τι ἂν αὕτη περιθῇ καλῶς ἀγωνίζεσθαι. ναυαγὸς
γέγονας, εὖ τὸν ναυαγόν· πένης ἐξ εὐπόρου, εὖ    5
τὸν πένητα·

        ἄρμενος ἐν μικροῖσι καὶ ἄρμενος ἐν
                    μεγάλοισιν·

ἀρκούμενος καὶ ἐσθῆτι τῇ τυχούσῃ καὶ διαίτῃ καὶ
διακονίᾳ, ὥσπερ ὁ Λαέρτης /                        10

        γρηὶ σὺν ἀμφιπόλῳ, ἥ οἱ βρῶσίν τε πόσιν τε
        παρτίθει·

καὶ ἐκοιμᾶτο χαμαὶ ἐπὶ στιβάδος·

        φύλλων κεκλιμένων χθαμαλαὶ βεβλήατο εὐναί.

ἀρκεῖ γὰρ ταῦτα καὶ εἰς τὸ προσηνῶς καὶ εἰς    15
τὸ ὑγιεινῶς, ἐὰν μή τις τρυφᾶν βούληται·
                  οὐ γὰρ ἐν γαστρὸς βορᾷ
    τὸ χρηστὸν εἶναι

οὐδέ γε ἐν χλανίδος κατασκευῇ οὐδὲ ἐν στρωμνῆς
μαλακότητι. οὐκ ἀηδῶς γὰρ Εὐριπίδης            20
                τρυφῇ δέ τοι
      πολλῶν ἐδεστῶν μηχανὰς θηρεύομεν·

καὶ οὐ μόνον ἐδεστῶν, ἀλλὰ καὶ ὀσφραντῶν καὶ
ἀκουστῶν. οὐ δεῖ δὲ τρυφᾶν οὐδὲν τῶν πραγμάτων μὴ φερόντων, ἀλλ᾽ ὥσπερ οἱ ναυτικοὶ    25
πρὸς τοὺς ἀνέμους καὶ πρὸς τὴν περίστασιν
ὁρῶντες· ἐκποιεῖ, χρῆσαι· οὐκ ἐκποιεῖ, παῦσαι.
καὶ ὥσπερ ἐπὶ στρατείας ὁ μὲν ἵππον ἔχων ἱππεὺς
ἀγωνίζεται, ὁ δὲ ὅπλα ὁπλίτης, ὁ δὲ μηδὲν /

# VI

## On Circumstances[1]

Fortune, like some poetess,[2] creates roles of
every kind: the shipwrecked man, the poor man, the
exile, the man of repute, the man without repute.
A good man must therefore play well any part she
assigns him.  You have been shipwrecked, play the
shipwreck well.  From a prosperous man you have become poor, play the poor man well:

> Equipped in adversity and equipped in
>                              prosperity[3]

being satisfied with any chance[4] garment, diet,
service, like Laertes[5]

> With an old servant woman who served him
>                              his food and drink[6]

And he would sleep upon a mattress on the ground:

> his humble bed was strewn with fallen
>                              leaves.[7]

For these things suffice for living calmly and in
good health, unless one wants to live in luxury:

> For not in the belly's glut
> lies the good.[8]

nor in the condition of a fine woolen garment, nor
in the softness of a mattress.  For not ineptly did
Euripides say:[9]

> From luxury, of course,
> We search out means for great amounts of
>                              foods.

And not only foods, but also for things to smell
and hear.  But one must certainly not try to live
in luxury if conditions do not permit it, but like
sailors[10] looking to the winds and circumstance:
if favorable, use them; if not favorable, stop.
And as on a campaign the man with a horse fights as
a horseman, the man with arms fights as a hoplite,

(54H)  ἔχων ψιλός, καὶ ὥσπερ ἐκεῖσε ὅταν ἐπικέωνται    30
οἱ πολέμιοι καὶ βάλλωσιν, εἰς τὰ ὅπλα ἀναχω-
ρεῖς ψιλὸς ὤν· οὕτως αὖ δεῦρο ἐπίκειται ἐνίοτε
πόλεμος, ἀπορία ἀρρωστία, ἀναχώρει εἰς μονο-
σιτίαν, εἰς αὐτοδιακονίαν, εἰς τρίβωνα, ἔσχατον
εἰς ᾅδου.    35

(54H)   while the man with nothing fights as a light-armed
        soldier; and just as when the enemy charge in that
        direction and hurl their weapons, you retreat to
        camp[11] since you are light-armed, so sometimes war
        presses upon one:[12] scarcity, sickness; retreat to
        one meal a day, to taking care of yourself, to a
        threadbare coat,[13] finally to Hades' realm.

## VII

Περὶ ἀπαθείας

Μήποθ᾽ ὃν τρόπον ἀπύρηνος ῥοὰ λέγεται καὶ
ἀτράχηλοι καὶ ἄπλευροι ἄνθρωποι, οὕτω καὶ
ἄλυποι καὶ ἄφοβοι ἄνθρωποι λέγονται;

Βούλει οὖν τοῖς αὐτοῖς παραδείγμασι
χρησάμενοι λέγωμεν, ὃν τρόπον ἀπύρηνος ῥόα     5
λέγεται καὶ ἄπλευροι καὶ ἀτράχηλοι ἄνθρωποι,
οὕτω καὶ ἀναμάρτητοι καὶ ἄφθονοι λέγονται;
καὶ ὃν τρόπον ἐκεῖ ἄπλευρος οὐ κατὰ στέρησιν
πλευρῶν, ἀλλὰ τοιούτων πλευρῶν λέγεται, οὕτω
καὶ ὁ ἄφρων καὶ ὁ ἄνους οὐ κατὰ στέρησιν     10
φρενῶν καὶ νοῦ, ἀλλὰ τοιούτων φρενῶν καὶ
τοιούτου νοῦ; καὶ ὥσπερ τὸν ἄπλευρον ἔχειν
μὲν φαμὲν πλευράς, μοχθηρὰς δέ, οὕτω καὶ τὸν
ἄνουν ἔχειν μὲν νοῦν, μοχθηρὸν δέ, καὶ τὸν
ἄφρονα ἔχειν μὲν φρένας, μοχθηρὰς δέ; ἢ παντά-     15
πασι τὸ πεπεῖσθαι ταῦτα γελοῖον;

Ἀλλ᾽ ὥσπερ ἀναμάρτητος ὁ ἐκτὸς ἁμαρτίας,
καὶ ἄφθονος / καὶ ἀβάσκανος <ὁ ἐκτὸς φθόνου
καὶ βασκανίας>, καὶ ἀπερίεργος καὶ ἀμεμψίμοι-
ρος <ὁ> ἐκτὸς ἑκατέρου τούτων, οὕτω καὶ ἄλυπος     20
καὶ ἄφοβος <ὁ> ἐκτὸς λύπης καὶ φόβου; οὕτω γὰρ
καὶ εὐδαίμων ἔσται [ὁ] ἐκτὸς τοῦ πάθους καὶ
ταραχῆς ὤν. ὅστις δὲ ἐν ὀδύνῃ καὶ λύπῃ [ὢν]
καὶ φόβῳ ἐστί, πῶς ἂν ἐκεῖνος εὐαρεστοίη τῷ
βίῳ, ἢ μὴ εὐαρεστῶν πῶς ἂν εἴη εὐδαίμων; ἢ     25
εἰ λύπῃ ἅψεται, πῶς οὐ καὶ φόβος καὶ ἀγωνία
καὶ ὀργὴ καὶ ἔλεος; ὧν γὰρ ὑπαρξάντων ἄνθρωποι
λυποῦνται, τούτων ἐν προσδοκίᾳ γενόμενοι
φοβοῦνται καὶ ἀγωνιῶσι καὶ τοὺς ἀναξίως
δοκοῦντας περιπίπτειν τούτοις     30

## VII

### On Freedom from Passion[1]

Perhaps in the same way that a pomegranate is called "seedless,"[2] and people "neckless" and "chestless," people are called "painless" and "fearless"?

So do you want us to use the same examples and say that as the pomegranate is called "seedless" and people "chestless" and "neckless" so they are called "blameless" and "ungrudging"? And just as in the other example the man is called "chestless," not because of a lack of chest, but from its nature, so a man is called "senseless" and "mindless," not because of a lack of sense and mind, but from the nature of his sense and mind? And just as we say that the "chestless" man possesses a chest but a bad one, so also we say that a mindless man possesses a mind but a bad one, and the "senseless" man has sense but a bad one? Or is it completely absurd to insist on these points?[3]

(56H) But just as the blameless man is the one beyond blame, and the ungrudging and unenvious man <is the one beyond grudging and envy>, and the incurious[4] and uncomplaining man <is the one> beyond either of these things, so a painless and fearless man <is the one> beyond pain and fear? For thus the happy man will also be the one beyond passion and disturbance. But whoever is in distress and pain and fear, how could he be satisfied[5] with life or if he is not satisfied how could he be happy? Or if distress touches him, how could fear and anguish and anger and compassion fail to do so? For when these conditions exist, men are pained; when they anticipate them, they are afraid and in anguish; and for those who seem to have fallen into

64

ἐλεοῦσι καὶ τοῖς κατὰ προαίρεσιν περιβάλλου-
σιν ὀργίζονται καὶ θυμοῦνται καὶ ὑφορῶνται·
καὶ οὓς μισοῦσι, τούτους ὁρῶντες εὖ πράττοντας
ζηλοτυποῦσι καὶ φθονοῦσι, καὶ ἀκούσαντες ἔχον-
τάς τι κακὸν ἐπιχαίρουσιν. εἰ οὖν ἐν λύπῃ      35
ἔσται, πῶς ἐκτός τινος ἔσται πάθους; ἢ μηθενὸς
ἐκτὸς ὢν πῶς ἀπαθὴς ἔσται;

     Ὅπερ δεῖ τὸν μακάριον εἶναι, ὥστε οὖν
μήτε ἐπὶ φίλου μήτε ἐπὶ τέκνου τελευτῇ λυπηθῆ-
(57H)  ναι, / εἴπερ μηδὲ ἐπὶ τῇ αὐτοῦ. ἢ οὐκ ἄναν-      40
δροί σοι δοκοῦσιν εἶναι οἱ τὸν ἑαυτῶν θάνατον
ἀγεννῶς καὶ μὴ εὐθαρσῶς προσδεχόμενοι; ἢ οὐ
δεῖ τὸν εὔψυχον καὶ ἀνδρεῖον εὐψύχως τὴν
ἑαυτοῦ τελευτὴν φέρειν, ὥσπερ Σωκράτης, μὴ
δυσφοροῦντα μηδὲ δυσκολαίνοντα; ἢ δυσχερέσ-      45
τερόν τι κρίνειν τὴν ἄλλου τελευτὴν τῆς ἑαυτοῦ;
ἢ οὐχ ὁμοίως αὐτὸν ἀγαπᾷ καὶ στέργει; ἢ τὸν
φίλον μᾶλλον καὶ τὰ τέκνα ἢ ἑαυτόν;

     Καὶ ταύτην μὲν ἐπαινοῦσιν ἐντελλομένην

        σὺ δ᾽ ὦ τεκοῦσα, μή τι σὴν      50
λιβάσι κατάσπενδε...........παρηΐδα,

τὴν δὲ κατακολουθοῦσαν ὠμὴν φησὶν ἡ δόξα.
ἐπεὶ καὶ ταυτασὶ τὰς Λακωνικὰς γυναῖκας πᾶς
τις ἐπαινεῖ ὡς εὐψύχους. ἀκούσασά <τις> τὸν
ἑαυτῆς υἱὸν σεσωσμένον καὶ πεφευγότα ἐκ τῶν      55
πολεμίων, γράφει αὐτῷ [κακὰ φάμα τεῦ κακκέχυ-
ται· τὺ ὦν ἢ ταύταν ἀπότριψαι ἢ μηδ᾽ ἀμῖν
φάνευ.] οὐχ ὡς ἂν Ἀττικὴ γυνὴ ἀκούσασα /
(58H)  σεσωσμένον ἔγραψεν ἂν 'εὖ τέκνον, ὅτι σαυτόν
μοι ἔσωσας,' ἀλλ᾽ ἐκ τῶν ἐναντίων      60

these things undeservedly they feel compassion; and
for those who become involved by choice they feel
anger, and are incensed and suspicious.  And those
whom they hate, when they see them prospering, they
are envious and spiteful; and when they hear that
they are having some misfortune, they gloat.  If,
then, he is to be in pain, how is he to be beyond
some passion?  Or being beyond no passion, how is
he to be free from passion?

Therefore, he should be a happy man, so that
he is not pained over the death either of a friend
(57H)   or a child, nor even over his own death.[6]  Or don't
those people seem to you cowardly who await their
own death ignobly and not at all boldly?  Or isn't
it necessary for the courageous and brave man to
bear his own death courageously, like Socrates, who
was not troubled or troublesome?  Or is it more
vexing to distinguish someone else's death from
one's own?  Or doesn't he love and feel affection
for himself in like fashion?  Or does he feel more
love and affection for his friend and children than
for himself?

And they commend this woman who commands[7]

But you, O mother, wet not
Your cheek with streams...

But popular opinion says that the woman obeying
this advice is hard-hearted.[8]  Whereas everyone
commends as courageous such Laconian women as
these:[9] <one>, hearing that her son had been saved
and had fled from the enemy,[10] writes to him ["an
evil report has been spread about you.  So you
either wipe it out or do not come into our
sight."][11] not as a woman of Attica on hearing
(58H)   that her son was safe, would write "well done,
child, because you have saved yourself for me."
But the Laconian woman's sentiment is the opposite:

'κακὰ φάμα τεῦ κακκέχυται· τὺ ὦν ἢ ταύταν
ἀπότριψαι ἢ μηδ' ἀμῖν φαίνευ,' τοῦτο δέ ἐστιν
'ἄπαγξαι.'

Καὶ ἄλλη πάλιν ἀπαγγείλαντος αὐτῇ τοῦ
κήρυκος ὅτι ὁ υἱὸς ἐν τῇ παρατάξει τετελεύ-      65
τηκε 'ποῖός τις' φησί 'γενόμενος;' 'ἀνὴρ
ἀγαθός, ὦ μῆτερ.' 'εὖγε, ὦ τέκνον' φησί·
'τούτου γὰρ ἕνεκά σε' φησίν 'ἐγέννησα, ἵνα
χρήσιμος καὶ βοηθὸς ἦσθα τᾷ Σπάρτᾳ.' οὐκ
ἔκλαιε καὶ ἐδεινοπάθει, ἀλλὰ καὶ ἀκούσασα ὅτι      70
εὐψύχως, ἐπῄνεσε.

Καὶ ἐκείνη δὲ πάλιν ἡ Λάκαινα ὡς γεννική·
φυγόντων γὰρ αὐτῆς τῶν υἱῶν ἐκ τῆς μάχης καὶ
παραγενομένων πρὸς αὐτὴν 'ποῦ' φησίν 'ἥκατε
φεύγοντες; ἢ δεῦρο καταδυσόμενοι ὅθεν ἐξέδυτε;'      75
ἀνασυραμένη καὶ δείξασα αὐτοῖς. ὅρα εἰ καὶ τῶν
(59H)  παρ' ἡμῖν τις γυναικῶν τοῦτ' ἂν / ποιήσειεν.
ἀλλ' οὐκ ἀσμένη ὄψεται σεσωσμένους; ἐκεῖναι
δ' οὔ. ἀλλ' ἀποθανόντας εὐψύχως ἥδιον...καὶ
ἐπιγράφουσι Λακεδαιμόνιοι      80

...οὔ[τε] τὸ ζῆν θέμενοι καλὸν οὔτε τὸ
                                    θνῄσκειν,
ἀλλα τὸ ταῦτα καλῶς ἀμφότερ' ἐκτελέσαι.

πῶς δὲ οὐκ ἀλόγιστον καὶ ἄλλως μάταιον τὸ
τελευτήσαντος τοῦ φίλου καθῆσθαι κλαίοντα καὶ      85
λυπούμενον καὶ ἑαυτὸν προσκαταφθείροντα; δέον,
ἵνα καί τι μᾶλλον φιλόσοφος δόξῃ παρὰ τοῖς
ἀποπλήκτοις, πρὸ τοῦ τελευτῆσαι τὸν φίλον
ὀδυνᾶσθαι <καὶ> κλαίειν, ἐνθυμούμενον ὅτι
αὐτῷ ὁ φίλος θνητὸς ἐγένετο καὶ ἄνθρωπος.      90
οὐ γὰρ ὀρθῶς φησὶ βουλευομένου ὁ Στίλπων τὸ
διὰ τοὺς ἀπογενομένους τῶν ζώντων ὀλιγωρεῖν·
γεωργὸς οὐ ποιεῖ τοῦτο, οὐδ' ἐὰν τῶν δένδρων
ξηρόν τι γένηται, καὶ τὰ ἄλλα προσεκκόπτει,
ἀλλὰ τῶν λοιπῶν ἐπιμελόμενος πειρᾶται τὴν      95
(60H)  τοῦ ἐκλελοιπότος χρείαν / ἀναπληροῦν.

"An evil report has been spread about you. So you
either wipe it out or do not come into our sight,"
that is to say, "be hanged."[12]

And again, another woman,[13] when the messenger
reported to her that her son had died in the battle, asked "How did he conduct himself?" "As a
brave man, mother." "Well done, child," she said.
"For this purpose," she said,[14] "I bore you: to be
useful and helpful to Sparta." She did not weep
and complain loudly of her sufferings, but hearing
that he died nobly, she commended him.[15]

And again,[16] that famous Laconian woman, how
noble! For when her sons fled from the battle and
came to her, she said, "Where have you come in your
flight? Is it to dive back in here where you came
from?" And she pulled up her clothing and showed
them. Consider if any of our women would do this.[17]
(59H) Instead, wouldn't they be glad to see their sons
saved? But not those other women. Instead, for
those who have died courageously the Lacedaemonians
gladly...[18] and set up inscriptions,[19]

> ...not counting living or dying an honor
> but fulfilling both of these with honor.

But how is it not illogical, and futile as well, to
sit weeping and grieving and even destroying oneself over the friend who has died? One should, in
order to appear more of a philosopher in the presence of those numb with grief, feel pain and weep
before the friend has died, reflecting that the
friend was born mortal and a human being.[20] For,
as Stilpon says, neglecting the living because of
the dead is the mark of a man who does not reason
correctly.[21] A farmer doesn't do this. He does
not, if one of his trees becomes withered, chop
down the rest. Instead he tends those that are
(60H) left and tries to compensate for the one that has
died.[22]

Οὐδ᾿ ἡμεῖς ἐπὶ τῶν ἡμετέρων μερῶν·
γελοῖον γὰρ ἔσται εἰ ἐὰν τὸν ἕτερόν τις
ὀφθαλμὸν ἀποβάλῃ, δεήσει καὶ τὸν ἕτερον
προσεκκόψαι, κἂν ὁ εἷς ποὺς κυλλός, καὶ τὸν      100
ἕτερον ἀνάπηρον ποιεῖν, κἂν ἕνα ὀδόντα, καὶ
τοὺς ἄλλους προσεκλέξαι· ἀλλ᾿ ἐπὶ μὲν τούτων
εἴ τις οὕτως οἴοιτο, μαργίτης.

Τοῦ δὲ υἱοῦ τελευτήσαντος ἢ τῆς γυναικός,
<εἰκὸς> αὐτοῦ τε ὀλιγωρεῖν ζῶντος καὶ τὰ ὑπάρ-    105
χοντα προσκαταφθείρειν; καὶ εἰ μὲν τῶν γνωρί-
μων τινὸς υἱὸς ἢ γυνὴ ἀπέθανε, παρεκάλεις ἄν,
οἰόμενος δεῖν ἀνδρωδῶς καὶ θαρσαλέως καὶ μὴ
βαρέως φέρειν· αὐτὸς δὲ τοῖς αὐτοῖς περιπεσὼν
συμπτώμασιν, οὕτως οἴει δεῖν δυσφορεῖν ἀλλ᾿    110
οὐ πράως. καὶ εἴπερ ἕτερον, παρακαλεῖν μέτριον ἐν στενοχωρίᾳ καὶ ἀπορίᾳ μὴ δυσκολαίνειν
μηδὲ ἀβίωτον τὸν βίον νομίζειν, ἀλλὰ τῷ
δοκοῦντι κακῷ τὸ δοκοῦν ἀγαθὸν ἀντιτιθέναι
καὶ ἐξισοῦν 'ἀπογέγονεν ὁ φίλος,' 'καὶ γὰρ     115
γέγονε.' σὺ δέ, ὅτι μὲν ἀπογέγονεν, ἀκληρεῖν
οἴει, ὅτι δὲ ἐγένετο, οὐκ εὐκληρεῖν· καὶ εἰ
(61H) μὲν μηκέτι παρέξεται χρείας ἀπο/γενόμενος,
ἄθλιον, ὅτι δὲ παρείχετο γενόμενος, οὐ μακά-
ριον.                                           120

Ναί· ἀλλ᾿ οὐκέτι ἔσται.

Οὐδὲ γὰρ ἦν μυριοστὸν ἔτος, οὐδ᾿ ἐπὶ τῶν
Τρωικῶν· οὐδὲ γὰρ κατὰ τοὺς προπάππους σου.
σὺ δὲ ἐπὶ μὲν τούτῳ οὐκ ἄχθῃ, ὅτι δὲ εἰς
ὕστερον οὐκ ἔσται, δυσχεραίνεις.              125

Χρειῶν γὰρ ἐστέρημαι.

---

110-111: On the words ἀλλ᾿...ἕτερον Hense remarks *nondum
expedita*, but cf. note 28.
115-116: Hense makes ἀπογέγονεν...γέγονε one saying. For
the change in punctuation cf. note 30.

Nor do we do this with the parts of our body.
For if[23] someone loses an eye, it will be absurd if
he asks that the other be cut out as well; and if
one foot is a club-foot, he mutilates[24] the other;
and if one tooth is pulled, he pulls out the rest
as well. Indeed, if anyone should think like this
over these matters, he would be a madman.[25]

But when your son or wife dies, <are you
likely>[26] to neglect your own living and destroy
your possessions as well? And if the son or wife
of one of your neighbors were to die, you would
console him,[27] feeling that he should bear it in a
manly and courageous manner and not be distressed.
But when you encounter the same misfortune yourself, you feel that you should be distressed, and
in no calm manner at that.[28] And you feel that if
another man is distressed you should encourage him
to be moderate[29] in his trouble and not to be dis-
traught over his loss or to consider life unlivable,
but[30] against the apparent evil to balance the apparent good and to equate "my friend has died" with
"for he has lived." But you consider yourself un-
fortunate because he has died but not because he
has lived; and because he is gone and will no long-
(61H) er provide friendship, you consider yourself
wretched, but not happy because he provided it
while he was alive.

Certainly! But he will no longer exist.

Nor, indeed, did he exist ten thousand years
ago, nor in Trojan times, nor even in the genera-
tion of your great-grandfathers. Yet you are not
grieved over this; rather you are distressed because he will not exist into later times.[31]

Yes, because I have been deprived of his
friendship.

Καὶ γὰρ ὑπουργιῶν, ἃς αὐτὸς ἐλειτούργεις
ζῶντι τῷ τέκνῳ καὶ τῷ φίλῳ καὶ κακοπαθῶν καὶ
δαπανῶν.

    "Αδηλον γὰρ φησὶν ὁ Σωκράτης οὐ μόνον τῷ     130
καλὴν <γήμαντι> εἰ ἐπὶ ταύτῃ πλείω, ἀλλὰ καὶ
τῷ τέκνα καὶ φίλους <ἔχοντι> εἰ περὶ τούτους
πλείω.

    "Επειτα δὴ καὶ ἀποδημοῦντος αὐτοῦ χρειῶν
στερηθῇ καὶ στρατευομένου ὑπὲρ τῆς πατρίδος     135
καὶ πρεσβεύοντος καὶ ἱερεύοντος καὶ ἀρρωστή-
σαντος καὶ πρεσβυτέρου γενομένου. ἀλλ' εἰ
ἐπὶ πᾶσι τούτοις δυσκολαίνοις, τί τοῖς γρα-
δίοις ἀπολείψεις;

    "Αλογον δὲ καὶ ἄμα μὲν ἐπιβάλλουσαν     140
ἡγεῖσθαι τὴν στρατείαν καὶ τὴν ἀποδημίαν τῷ
φίλῳ καὶ αὐτὸν συνεκπίπτειν καὶ εἰ μὴ ἀποδη-
(62H) μοίη ἐγκαλεῖν ὡς / ἁμαρτάνοντι, ἄμα δὲ δυσφορεῖν εἰ ἀποδημήσει ἢ στρατεύσεται. καλῶς τὸ
τοῦ κυβερνήτου ἐκείνου 'ἀλλ' οὖν γε, ὦ Πόσει-     145
δον, ὀρθήν.' οὕτω καὶ ἀνὴρ ἀγαθὸς εἴποι πρὸς
τὴν τύχην 'ἀλλ' οὖν γε ἄνδρα, καὶ οὐ βλᾶκα.'

---

127:     ἐλειτούργεις Jacobs] ἐλειτούργει MSS.  Cf. note
        32.
131-132:  γήμαντι...ἔχοντι  I have lifted from Jacobs'
        elaborate attempt to complete the sense of this
        passage.  See note 34 and Hense's apparatus.

And also of the services which you yourself[32] used to render to the son and the friend by your hardships and expenditures.

For, says Socrates,[33] it is unclear whether the man who marries a beautiful woman will have any advantage in her and in the same way whether the man who has children and friends will have any advantage in their case.[34]

But then, too, while he is abroad you will be deprived of his friendship,[35] and while[36] he is serving his country on a military campaign, and as ambassador, while he is sacrificing,[37] when he becomes ill, and when he has grown older. But if you should be distressed over all these matters, what will you leave for the old hags?

(62H)  But it is quite illogical at one moment to consider military service and travel abroad incumbent on a friend--and to think that he agrees[38]--and if he does not go abroad to criticize him for doing wrong, yet at another moment to feel distress if he goes abroad or serves on a campaign. Quite to the point was the utterance of that pilot: "At any rate,[39] Poseidon, on an even keel."[40] So also a good man might say to Fortune, "At any rate a man and not a stupid one."[41]

## NOTES TO THE TRANSLATION

### I

[1]D. R. Dudley (*A History of Cynicism*, p. 86) translates the opening sections of this piece and concludes
with the remark that "However edifying this may have been
to the youth of Megara, it is deficient in both literary
and logical virtues." Dudley's appraisal is close to the
mark, but many of us have the same feeling about his book.

[2]This little sentence is awkward and obscure.

[3]On the subject of "goods," cf. III.9-36 where Teles
quotes Stilpon. There the "goods" are divided, as here,
into three categories: "goods" of the soul, "goods" of the
body, and external "goods." See also II.27ff.

[4]Cf. Plutarch, *On Love of Wealth* Ch. 1, 523D for a
similar list.

[5]For a description of this man's position and its
importance in an ancient army, cf. Thucydides V. 71, 1.

[6]Teles seems to have Sophocles *Aias* 961f. in mind.
The verb ἐπιχαίρω occurs but twice in Sophocles' extant
plays: *Aias* 136, 961. In the first passage the word has a
good sense, in the latter a bad sense.

[7]Cf. Aeschines, *Against Ctesiphon* 16 and Plutarch's
use of the passage in his *On Stoic Contradictions* ch. 2,
1033C-D. For parallels, see Cherniss' note in Loeb *Mor-
alia* XIII B, p. 413, note e. To these parallels, add
Epictetus, *Ench.* 13, 17, and perhaps 33.

### II

[1]Cf. Epictetus, *Ench.* 17.

[2]Cf. Teles VI.1.

[3]Neither πρωτολόγος nor δευτερολόγος occurs elsewhere. Many books on Greek drama use the terms πρωταγωνίστης and δευτεραγωνίστης to identify the first and second actor, but as A. W. Pickard-Cambridge points out (*The
Dramatic Festivals of Athens*, Oxford, 1953, pp. 133-36),
these terms are not used in reference to actors in any
extant writing before Plutarch. He uses πρωταγωνίστης in
this sense (*Political Praecepts* ch. 21, 816F) and πρωταγω-
νιστεῖν in the sense of "to be a πρωταγωνίστης" in his
*Life of Lysander* ch. 23, 336d. Teles, however, may give

us an indication that these terms were not yet in regular use in his day. Notice that in line 2 he uses the verb ἀγωνίζεσθαι. One would expect that the use of this verb would have led logically to his writing πρωταγωνίστης and δευτεραγωνίστης if these terms had been in current use.

[4]Cf. Teles III.58-61.

[5]Cf. Plutarch, *On Love of Wealth* ch. 10, 528B.

[6]Cf. Teles III.43 for a similar phrase.

[7]Cf. Athenaeus III. 114F which make it clear that this is a barley cake for which the meal is not finely ground. Cf. Aristophanes, *Wasps* 610.

[8]This sentence closely resembles Xenophon, *Memorabilia* I. 6, 5.

[9]Cf. Teles IVA.127-129.

[10]The παρθενών was a chamber in various Greek temples, e.g., the Parthenon at Athens, the temple of Artemis at Magnesia on the Maeander, the temple of the Great Mother at Cyzicus.

[11]Cf. Epictetus, *Ench*. 5.

[12]This line is quoted by Plutarch in his *On Tranquility* ch. 18, 477A. See Helmbold's remark in the Loeb edition, vol. VI, p. 237, note a. The general context of Plutarch's passage resembles Teles' (i.e., Bion's) remarks.

[13]There is an extended play on words in this passage that must be attributed to Bion rather than Teles. Notice παρὰ τὴν λῆψιν (56-57) and παρὰ τὴν ὑπόληψιν (59-60). The latter word is picked up by ὑπολάβῃς (61) which in turn echoes ἐπιλαμβάνῃ (58). It is, of course, almost impossible to retain these puns in English.

[14]In addition to the problem caused by the pun, there is also the matter of a correct interpretation of ὑπόληψις. Epictetus (*Ench*. 1) lists this term as the first in a group of four things which are under our control: ἐφ᾽ ἡμῖν μὲν ὑπόληψις, ὁρμή, ὄρεξις, ἔκκλισις καὶ ἑνὶ λόγῳ ὅσα ἡμέτερα ἔργα. The order of the four terms is not accidental, for they depict a person's mental activities from the original conception to the final rejection. Epictetus uses the word in a positive, or at least neutral, sense. In other writers, however, it seems to possess a near pejorative sense, e.g., Sextus Empiricus *Against the Logicians* II (= *Against the Mathematicians* VII) 432: πᾶσα φαύλου κατ᾽ αὐτοὺς ὑπόληψις ἀγνοία ἐστι. See also Plutarch, *On Stoic Contradictions*, 1056a; Marcus Aurelius

VIII. 40. Such a negative connotation seems implied by Teles, hence the translation "wrong assumption."

[15]Cf. Epictetus, *Ench*. 5.

[16]Cf. Teles VI.25ff.

[17]Hense and his precursors, usually ready to alter the text on the slightest pretext, have been strangely reluctant to discard a word which makes no sense. μεθείλαντο is a rare form of μεθαιρέομαι, and this verb had no meaning that can even remotely fit the sense of the passage. Hense, however, follows Cobet in understanding the verb to equal μεταβάλλειν or ἀλλάττειν, but no one has explained how μεθαιρέομαι can have this meaning, nor has a parallel been offered in proof. The only possible justification for retaining μεθείλαντο is the seemingly deliberate assonance of ἐστείλαντο, μεθείλαντο. But deliberate on whose part: Teles or Theodorus or Stobaeus or some scribe? But still, what can the word mean? Assonance alone is not enough; the word must make some sense. In the parallel passage (VI.25-27), when the wind is unfavorable the sailors stop (παῦσαι). What is the logical action here where the discussion centers on the idea of making the best of one's situation? Furl the sails and ride out the adverse conditions. Obviously ἐστείλαντο (sc. τὰ ἄρμενα) supplies the first idea, μεθείλαντο does not supply the second. There are probably several words that can give a satisfactory sense, but the closest palaeographically is μεθεῖντο. μεθίημι has several nuances that can be applied here: it can be a virtual synonym of παῦσαι in VI.27 and, though rare, it has the meaning of giving the ship its head. See Sophocles *Aias* 250 (and Jebb's note). It is possible even to find an explanation for the corruption here. Someone, reading ἐστείλαντο, μεθεῖντο, deliberately or accidentally produced the assonance by inserting -λα-, thus creating the impossible μεθείλαντο.

[18]Another impossible reading. Again Hense tries to defend the indefensible, but no explanation can justify πρὸς τὰ παρόντα χρῶ. Buecheler suggested adding ὅρα, and this seems the easiest solution.

[19]Hense may be correct in accepting Wilamowitz's deletion of these words.

[20]There appears to be no parallel to this meaning of κίων, but the context requires it, and the pun in προστάς (line 79), a frequent word for prostitution, seems to reinforce the idea.

[21]The puns here, on meaning and sound, are almost untranslatable.

[22]See *Sym*. IV. 35 where the wording is somewhat different.

[23]Plutarch relates a similar incident about Socrates in *On Tranquility* ch. 10, 470F. Cf. Juvenal *Sat*. III. 183-184: *omnia Romae/cum pretio*.

[24]Something is wrong with the text, for these words do not make a complete sentence.

[25]For the perfume called Kypros, see Theophrastus' *De odoribus* 25 where we learn how it was made.

[26]The χοῖνιξ represented the daily allowance of grain or bread.

[27]Cf. Plutarch, *Can Vice Cause Unhappiness?* ch. 3, 499c.

[28]This whole sentence seems obscure. The translation may be wrong.

[29]This is a very difficult passage. The general sense seems clear, but the precise meaning is obscure in several places. In addition, there are puns that defy translation and apparent ellipses that resist completion. In particular, ὥστε in lines 142 and 143 seems virtually impossible after ῥᾴδιον unless something is supplied to allow the conjunction to introduce a result clause. Then there is the phrase ἀλλὰ τὸν αὐτοῦ ἀμφότερα. What noun should be understood with αὐτοῦ and ἀμφότερα?

[30]LSJ lists this passage (s.v. ἄφορτος) but suggests ἀφόρτως φέρειν, "to bear easily." To understand φέρειν out of ἐγεγκόντα (line 137) is surely impossible, especially since the dative τῷ πλούτῳ is here. It is the appropriate form of χράομαι that must be supplied from χρῶνται (line 140).

[31]The phrase ἔμβα πορθμίδος ἔρυμα is strange. It is probably a quotation from some poet, for the accusative with ἐμβαίνω is a poetic construction. Nauck suggested that it was part of a quotation from Timotheus (frag. 11b of Wilamowitz) but Hense disagrees, and Page (*Poetae Melici Graeci*, frag. 10, p. 402) sides with Hense. It is probable, however, that the poem of Timotheus touched upon the same theme which is not uncommon. Cf., for example, Epictetus, *Ench*. 7.

[32]Some such verb as ὑποκρίνεται or πράττει seems to have fallen from the text.

[33]Meineke has suggested an unnecessary lacuna here. For a parallel to this section, see Epictetus IV, 1, 159-169.

[34]Needless to say, Teles is confused. The judges did not propose a fine (cf. Plato, *Apol.* 37A), and there is no other reference to a three-day respite (cf. *Phaedo* 116E-117A), but, cf. Diogenes Laertius II. 35.

[35]These words give a rather free version of Plato, *Phaedo* 117B-C.

[36]Teles has again confused stories. Xenophon (*Hell.* II 3, 56), followed by Cicero (*Tusc. Disp.* I. 40, 96) relates the death of Theramenes, who offered the toast to Critias, the instigator of his execution. See Hense's discussion of this passage for other interesting connections between the various men here.

[37]This rather inane sentence may, as Cobet thought, be an interpolation or, as Diels suggested, an addition by Theodorus. Whatever the origin, both Xenophon and Cicero conclude their version of the story with a not dissimilar idea. In Xenophon μήτε τὸ φρόνιμον μήτε τὸ παιγνιῶδες ἀπολιπεῖν ἐκ τῆς ψυχῆς; in Cicero *lusit vir egregius extremo spiritu.*

[38]These sentences make little sense and seemingly have nothing to do with what has gone before, with what follows, or with one another. Hense was right to mark a lacuna at this point, but no defense (and he attempts one) can explain away the chaos of these three separate ideas.

[39]This anecdote seems not to occur elsewhere, but it agrees with the ancient tradition about both Socrates (e.g., Plutarch, *On Control of Anger*, ch. 4, 455A-B; ch. 10, 458C) and Xanthippe (e.g., Diogenes Laertius II. 36-37). In the latter passage, her scolding is compared with the rattle of a windlass and the cackle of geese.

[40]Cf. Plutarch, *On Control of Anger*, ch. 13, 461D, where the guest is Euthydemus, and *On Tranquility*, ch. 11, 471B where a similar story is told about Pittacus and his wife.

[41]The construction ταύτῃ πάσχειν seems to be unparalleled. The regular construction is τι ὑπό τινος πάσχειν.

[42]The meaning of γενναία is unclear. In Plutarch's version (see note 40) ὄρνις is not modified by an adjective, which is the case here in lines 202, 205, 206. Perhaps we should read γνησία ("real," "genuine").

[43]Teles is not always precise in his designation when two characters are involved, but the substitution of an occasional proper name in the translation can help to keep matters straight.

[44]Cf. Lucian, *Zeus Tragoedus* 15: ἀλεκτρυόνα... γέροντα...καὶ κορυζῶντα.

[45]Who is the subject of φησίν? As Hense punctuates, it must be Alcibiades, but the sense of the passage seems to require that Socrates speak these words.

[46]This inane remark may, as Hense and others have thought, be a naive attempt of Theodorus to get into the act.

## III

[1]Exile was a common subject for philosophical discussion among both the Greeks and the Romans. In particular, the works still extant, in whole or part, are those of Teles, Musonius, Plutarch, Favorinus, Seneca. There are also brief discussions in Epictetus, Cicero and others. Nor can we ignore Ovid's *Tristia* and *Epistulae ex Ponto*. There is, however, a remarkable similarity between the works of Teles, Musonius and Plutarch; so much so, in fact, that it is obvious the three men used the same or similar sources. See the Introduction to the Loeb edition (vol. VII, pp. 513-517) of Plutarch's *On Exile* and the bibliography listed there.

[2]There is an untranslatable pun in ἀλογιστοτέρους. It means "less skillful," "less intelligent," or "of less account." Notice that it is contrasted with εὐλογιστίας in line 11.

[3]βουλεύεσθαι is a strange word here, but it may anticipate εὐβουλία in line 66.

[4]See Hense (p. XLIX) for a discussion of this section. With the words τί λέγεις the writing (dialogue?) of Stilpon, which Teles claims to be quoting, begins. But where does it end? Hense thinks it ends on line 36 with the words ἐν τῇ ἰδίᾳ μένοντες. Certainly it must end before the reference to Lycinus in line 41, for the events referred to there happened almost a century after Stilpon's death. A more logical end is the remark of Themistocles in line 31. The next sentence (notice the emphatic position of νῦν δέ) dismisses older examples and brings the discussion down to Teles' own time.

[5]With this whole section, cf. Teles I.14-28.

[6]For a discussion of exile and whether it deprives a person of goods, see Musonius IX, p. 74, 21ff. (Lutz). For a discussion of goods of the soul and external goods, see Zeno's remarks in Diogenes Laertius VII. 95-96; cf. also Teles I, note 3.

[7]Cf. Musonius IX, p. 70, 10-22.

[8]Zeno (Diogenes Laertius VII. 95) defines the external goods: τὰ δ' ἐκτὸς τό τε σπουδαίαν ἔχειν πατρίδα καὶ σπουδαῖον φίλον καὶ τὴν τούτων εὐδαιμονίαν.

[9]This is a rather obscure sentence. Musonius (IX. p. 70, 32-34) expresses the same idea more clearly: λέγω δὲ τούς γε λόγου ἀξίους ἄνδρας οὐ τῶν ἀναγκαιοτάτων μόνον πρὸς τὸν βίον ῥαδίως ἂν εὐπορεῖν ἔξω τῆς οἰκείας ὄντας, ἀλλὰ καὶ πολλὰ περιποιήσεσθαι χρήματα πολλάκις. Cf. Plutarch, *On Exile* ch. 7, 601F.

[10]A combination of *Iliad* IX. 479, 480, 483. Another example of the Cynic practice of tampering with texts for instructional purposes.

[11]There is, of course, a play on two meanings of ἀπόλλυμι: "to die" and "to be ruined." The anecdote is a favorite of Plutarch: cf. *Sayings of Kings and Commanders*, 185F; *On the Fortune of Alexander*, 328F; *On Exile*, 602A. Cf. also Musonius IX, p. 72, 3-6, where Themistocles' prosperity among the Persians is discussed but without a reference to this saying.

[12]Lycinus was an Italian exile, possible from Tarentum (so B. G. Niebuhr, *Kleine Schriften*, I, Bonn 1828, p. 461, who suggests that Lycinus fled from Tarentum when the Romans captured that city in 272/1 B.C.). In Greece he entered the service of Antigonus Gonatas and was appointed commander of the garrison at, perhaps, Megara. Whether he held this post before the Megarian uprising in the Chremonidean War or at its conclusion is uncertain. In either case, Teles refers here to an event that took place between 271 and 263 B.C.

[13]For the construction of τὸ προσταττόμενον ἐποιοῦμεν Λυκίνῳ see, for example, Demosthenes' *Against Macartatus* 59; cf. Teles II.25.

[14]Hippomedon was a Spartan, a son of Agesilaus and uncle of Agis IV. When his father was exiled in 241 B.C., Hippomedon went with him though he had not shared in the Spartan displeasure. It was at this time that he entered the service of Ptolemy Euergetes, for that Egyptian ruler had taken advantage of the situation resulting from the Third Syrian War to seize control, in 243 or 242 B.C., of the Seleucid territory in Europe, including parts of Thrace (cf. M. Cary, *The Greek World from 323 to 146 B.C.*, London[2] 1951, pp. 58f., 120f., 152ff.).

Thus we have another indication of the date for this selection of Teles, for he says in lines 45-46: ὁ νῦν ἐπὶ Θρᾴκης καθεσταμένος ὑπὸ Πτολεμαίου. See Hense's discussion, p. xxix.

[15]The Ptolemy here is Philadelphus, who stirred the Athenians into a revolt against Antigonus Gonatas in 267 B.C. and then failed to provide them with adequate support. The result was disaster for the Athenians (and, among others, their Megarian allies) in the so-called Chremonidean War, named after the Athenian leader Chremonides. For a discussion of Chremonides and Glaucon, see the Introduction and especially note 4.

Two notable deaths occurred at Athens during the Chremonidean War: That of the comic poet Philemon and that of the philosopher Zeno of Citium.

[16]Something is wrong with the text at this point, as most editors have realized. Who is the subject of ἐξαπεστάλη, etc.? Meineke suggested adding Χρεμωνίδης before καὶ χρημάτων. This is an ingenious idea and palaeographically feasible, but would even Teles drop Glaucon without further reference and concentrate upon just one of the two men? Perhaps we should put parentheses around Χρεμωνίδης ...σύμβουλοι, thus making Hippomedon the subject of ἐξαπεστάλη. But that sequence of examples is hardly less awkward than the present wording. That a fourth example is represented by this sentence is highly unlikely. Teles has already given three examples of men who fared better in exile than at home, and three is the regular number. If we knew more about the events referred to here, we could be in a better position to understand the reference. As it is, the best solution is to suggest that a lacuna exists before the words καὶ τὸ τελευταῖον.

[17]βάκηλοι is a strange word here. It is almost a technical term used to describe the eunuch priests of Cybele (cf. Lucian *Eun.* 8; *Sat.* 12; Zenobius *Ath.* 2.70). Yet according to Zenobius, Menander (frag. 477 Edmonds) used the word simply as a term of reproach. Zenobius explains it is αὕτη τέτακται κατὰ τῶν ἐκλύτων καὶ ἀνάνδρων ("This is used in regard to the nerveless and unmanly.")

[18]Another bit of strange Greek. The author contrasts the roles of σύ and ἐγώ, but he seems to get himself into a grammatical corner by using βασιλεύεις. To say that a paedagogus is king misses the mark, yet how else can the sentence be understood without taking γευόμενος as a dangling participle? The phrase καὶ τὸ τελευταῖον ἐμαυτοῦ is equally strange, but ἐμαυτοῦ probably depends on whatever verb is to be understood out of βασιλεύεις.

This whole sentence is very similar to another awkward passage: II.9-11: σὺ μὲν ἄρχεις καλῶς, ἐγὼ δὲ ἑνὸς τουτουῒ παιδαγωγὸς γενόμενος..., but at least this passage has the general term ἄρχω instead of the more specific βασιλεύω.

[19]Temple of Demeter which only women (and occasionally girls) could enter. The Thesmophorion meant here is the one at Megara, see note 20 below.

[20]According to Thucydides (IV.67), the temple of
Enyalius at Megara was the site of an Athenian ambush when
they attacked and captured that city in 424 B.C.   In his
commentary on this passage, A. W. Gomme (*Commentary on
Thucydides*, Oxford 1945, III. p. 529) says that the temple
has not been identified but that it probably stood near
the shore, just east of Nisaia.   Pausanias, in his description of Megara, does not mention such a temple although he identifies numerous temples of other deities,
including one of Demeter Thesmophorus (I.42,6) which he
saw on the second acropolis, called Alcathoe.   This is
probably the temple to which Teles refers.
      Despite the paucity of evidence about these two tem-
ples, I have found no commentary which cites this passage
of Teles.   Even W. Smith's *A Dictionary of Greek and Roman
Geography* omits any reference to Teles at this point.

[21]This is a strange sentence.   What is the noun to be
understood with παλαιστρικῇ?   Is it ἀλοιφῇ out of ἠλει-
φάμην?   But isn't this sort of ellipsis rather subtle for
an author who often repeats even non-essential words *ad
nauseam*?   There is a parallel, however, in IVA.122-124:
εἰ ἀλείφασθαι χρείαν ἔχοι, εἰσελθὼν ἂν εἰς τὸ βαλανεῖον τῷ
γλοιῷ ἠλείφατο.   Thus παλαιστρικῇ may be the same as ὁ
γλοιός.

[22]There is a play on the two meanings of ἄβατος here
and in line 73 above.   In the earlier line the word has
its derivative meaning of "holy place," (cf. R. G. Jebb,
*Sophocles Oedipus Coloneus*, reprinted Amsterdam 1962, comm.
to line 10) but here it has its basic sense of "cannot be
walked on."   There seems no way to retain both meanings,
and thus the pun, in English.

[23]Possibly another play on words.   εὐπλοεῖν insures
that νεώς is the genitive of ναῦς, but Teles has also been
discussing temples, and νεώς is also the genitive of ναός.
It is hard not to see an intended play on words here, especially when there is the play on ἄβατος and, perhaps, on
the sound and meaning of εὐπλοεῖν and εὐδαιμονεῖν.
εὐπλοεῖν commonly appears in the same metaphorical expres-
sion as the English "to have clear sailing," and that idea
frequently comes close to "being happy," i.e., εὐδαιμονεῖν.

[24]The two adjectives ἐπιεικής and δίκαιος can be an-
tonyms: "fair, equitable but not in strict observance of
the law" vs. "strict obedience to the δίκη."   For a discussion of these two terms, see Aristotle's *Nic. Eth*.
V.9,17-10,8, where the conclusion is reached that ταὐτὸν
ἄρα δίκαιον καὶ ἐπιεικές.   Yet even after this statement
Aristotle continues to compare and contrast the two terms.

[25]φησίν surely does not belong here: who is the subject?

[26]The reply is similar to Socrates' rejoinder to Apollodorus in Xenophon's *Apology* 28; cf. his reply to Xanthippe in Diogenes Laertius II. 35.

[27]Is there any significance to the repetition of such words as ἀκλήρημα (lines 82, 103, 107, 108), ἔγκλημα (line 94), εὐκλήρημα (line 109)?

[28]The shift of tenses is awkward. Why is ᾖσθου aorist while ἡγῇ and ἔχεις are present tense? And notice (cf. Hense's apparatus) that ἡγῇ σύ is Buecheler's emendation of ἡγήσῃ which appears in several manuscripts.

[29]ἐγένετο...καὶ ἐτράφη had, by Teles' day, probably become as much a cliché as our "born and bred." The phrase first appears in *Iliad* I. 251; cf. *Acts* 22:2.

[30]See Seneca's *Moral Epistle* 58,35: *prosiliam ex aedificio putri ac ruenti*. The context there, however, is different. The subject is suicide, and the house is the body. See, however, Teles II.149-158, where the same image of a house and life is used. As here, a metaphor of a ship follows.

[31]This is a clumsy metaphor expressed in clumsy language. The reference to a ship in the present context may, however, be an allusion to the "ship of state." Even so, to speak of someone being born on a ship and sailing on it from boyhood is stretching the metaphor to the breaking point (like the boy on the boat here).

[32]Hense's change of ἀπορρήγνυσθαι to διαρρήγνυσθαι may be unnecessary, but his reference to Aristophanes' *Frogs* 254-255 is clever and almost persuasive.

[33]All three places are, of course, small and relatively insignificant.

[34]αὐτήν (see Buecheler's emendation in the apparatus) seems better, but cf. Seneca's *Moral Epistle* 66, 26: *nemo enim patriam quia magna est amat, sed quia sua*.

[35]Nauck (*Trag. Graec. Frag.*: Adespota 536) does not include μέτοικε σύ as part of the verse quotation. Incidentally, this is the only place where the second speaker ventures to use a quotation to voice his objection to the argument.

[36]Hense cites pseudo-Plato's *Axiochus* 368D as the source of this reference, but the context is not very close to Teles' words. See the emendation suggested by Cobet.

[37]For the phrase, see Aeschylus' *Seven Against Thebes* 539, where the reference is to the Sphinx, the disgrace of Thebes.

[38]See Thucydides II.34,5: τιθέασιν οὖν ἐς τὸ δημόσιον σῆμα. Teles, however, is obviously playing on the sound and meaning of δημοκρατία and δημόσιος.

[39]Frag. 85 (Mannebach).

[40]See Diogenes Laertius IV.31 (= Anth. Planud. II. 383) where the second couplet seems to refer to the same idea and attributes it to a proverb: ὡς αἶνος ἀνδρῶν. Cicero (*Tusc. Disp.* I.104) attributes the same thought to Anaxagoras: *undique enim ad inferos tantumdem viae est*, but this passage has not been accepted as a fragment by Diels. See also Epictetus II. 6,18: τί σοι μέλει, ποίᾳ καταβῇς εἰς Ἅιδου; ἴσαι πᾶσαί εἰσιν.

[41]Euripides *Phoenissae* 1447-1451.

[42]See the apparatus.

[43]Nauck, *trag. gr. adesp.* 281, p. 893. Cf. Diogenes Laertius IV.25 where the line (with one change) is credited to Crantor.

[44]See Epictetus IV. 7.31: ἀλλ᾽ ἄταφος ῥιφήσῃ, and compare the whole discussion with that of Teles.

[45]See Theognis 833: πάντα τάδ᾽ ἐν κοράκεσσι καὶ ἐν φθόρῳ.

[46]For the thought, see Seneca's *Moral Epistle* 92,34; Petronius' Satyricon 115; Plutarch, *Can Vice Cause Unhappiness?* ch. 3, 499D.

[47]Euripides' *Phoenissae* 1451-1452.

[48]See Aeschylus' *Prometheus Bound* 316. Something is, however, clearly wrong with the text at this point. There are several problems: 1) What is the meaning and construction of ἡμετέρα? As Hense prints it, it must modify παιδιά, but this is a curious phrase; 2) The thought seems to jump, for what follows has little connection with these words; 3) ἰδεῖν and ἄψασθαι need an object.

[49]There is probably a lacuna here as well, for with no explicit reference to the Egyptians the final sentence of the selection is nonsense. It is, of course, possible that the Egyptians were mentioned in the passage which fell out to create the lacuna discussed in note 48.

[50]See Herodotus II.136,2, which seems to be the ultimate source of Teles' remark. Cicero (*Tusc. Disp.* I.45, 108 = *S.V.F.* III.322) quotes Chrysippus' reference to this custom of the Egyptians; cf. Sextus Empiricus, *Pyrrh.* III. 226.

[51]The selection seems incomplete, for there is no return to the subject of exile.

## IVA

[1]Stobaeus gives no title to this selection or to IVB, if indeed they are two pieces (cf. IVB, note 1). The subject, however, of both pieces is poverty and wealth, and so the title given by Frobenius is as good as any.

[2]Teles is confused or is, as Cynics were in the habit of doing, deliberately confusing matters. It was not Priam who refrained from sitting upon one of the seats but Penelope. These words and the verse immediately following came from *Odyssey* IV. 716-717 which describe Penelope's emotions when she learns that Telemachus has left Ithaca in search of his father.

[3]These words are echoed by Teles at VI.13 in a context where Laertes is the subject and where *Odyssey* I. 191-192 is quoted just as here (cf. note 5 below).

[4]These words are taken from *Iliad* XXII. 414, where we read of Priam's reaction to the death of Hector.

[5]Deleted by Meineke. Some copyist noticed the similarity between this passage and Teles VI.10-16 and decided to quote the Homeric lines here as well, not realizing that Teles himself alludes to them. These words are a combination of *Odyssey* XVIII. 358 and I. 191-192. Cf. note 3 above.

[6]Hense is correct in supposing that something has fallen from the text at this point.

[7]Cf. *Odyssey* XI. 591-592.

[8]The noun δυσελπιστία is, at first glance, a curious choice, and for that reason Meineke (see Apparatus) wanted to change it. The word is, however, correct. It occurs again in line 72 below and in the same context. Furthermore the same word appears as part of the same subject in [Aristotle's] *On Virtues and Vices* VII. 14, 1251b25: ἀκολουθεῖ δὲ τῇ μικροψυχίᾳ μικρολογία, μεμψιμοιρία, δυσελπιστία, ταπεινότης. Rackham (Loeb edition) translates this sentence "small-mindedness is accompanied by pettiness, querulousness, pessimism, self-abasement."

[9]The verb στραγγεύεται is a bit strange here, but it is clearly correct. There is an untranslatable pun between this verb and γεύονται in line 28 above.

[10]By "ancients" he refers to earlier Cynics. See Hense, p. XLVIII.

[11]τοῦτο is surely wrong.  Every other word in this passage which refers to money is plural: χρημάτων, αὐτά, ὄντα, but especially αὐτοῖς which refers to the same money as τοῦτο.  Thus ταῦτα should be read.

[12]ἐπὶ τοῦ παρόντος is a rare phrase.  See Hense's note and add Epictetus, *Ench.* 2.2.

[13]For the story of the Phorcides, cf. Apollodous II. 4, 2 and Frazer's note in the Loeb, Vol. I, p. 155.

[14]Plutarch gives a similar argument, but without the mythological element, in his *On Love of Wealth* ch. 7, especially 526B-C.

[15]A very curious passage.  The reference to fishes, doves and dogs is clear enough, for these animals were worshipped by certain peoples for whom their flesh was taboo (cf., for example, Sextus Empiricus *Pyrrh.* III. 220-226), while other peoples ate them.  But what about the skull of a man?  It was neither worshipped nor considered by anyone to be eatable.  Certainly the skull itself (κρανίον) could not be eaten.  Teles, or his source, is obviously confused, and the confusion may be the result of some statement of Diogenes who is reported to have said (Diogenes Laertius XI. 73) that there was nothing impious in τὸ καὶ τῶν ἀνθρωπείων κρεῶν ἅψασθαι.  Add to this the statement of "certain people" (probably Pythagoreans) that θᾶττον ἂν τὰς κεφαλὰς φαγεῖν...τῶν πατέρων ἢ κυάμους, and someone could have written the nonsensical statement that we read in Teles.  Of course all difficulties would be removed if κρέας were read instead of κρανίον, but how can the change from a logical to an illogical word be explained?

[16]Cf. note 10 above.

[17]At least from the time of Xenophon the pun on χρῆμα and κτῆμα, etc. was a favorite among the Greeks.  See Plutarch, *On Common Conceptions* ch. 20, 1068A and Cherniss' note in Loeb vol. XIII B, p. 725, note e.

[18]Cf. note 8 above.

[19]αὑτῷ is the emendation of Blass and is accepted by Hense in place of αὐτῷ.  Both men understand αὑτῷ to refer to ἄλλον, and perhaps it does.  Teles is not always logical in his use of pronouns.  But if αὐτῷ is correct, Teles is counseling against money in only one of the two situations which he mentions.  He says nothing about not seeking money to free oneself from scarcity.  Since τις is the agent in both situations, only αὑτῷ, which in effect refers to the agent, can take care of both men.

[20]Cf. Plutarch, *On Love of Wealth* ch. 3, 524C-D.

[21]οὗτος refers, of course, to ἄλλον (cf. note 19 above). This casual use of οὗτος (even ἐκεῖνος would have been preferable) is merely one more example of Teles' clumsy use of pronouns, a sure sign of an inexperienced writer.

[22]Superstition became a regular item in the Stoic catalogue of sins which result from wealth. See, for example, Horace's *Satire* II. 3; cf. Teles IVA.135ff.

[23]The reference to the Academy is interesting (cf. Dudley, *A History of Cynicism*, p. 47. He, too, seems confused). It may be a sign of a more serious problem here. In the discussion which follows, Metrocles first studied at the Lyceum and then went to Crates. In the present passage, the manuscripts name two opponents, the Academy and Crates. Could Teles, Theodorus or even Stobaeus have been confused and identified Theophrastus and Xenocrates with the Academy?

[24]Metrocles of Maroneia, the brother of Hipparchia, who became the wife of Crates. The chief source of our information about Metrocles is, in addition to Teles, Diogenes Laertius VI. 94 (cf. II. 102; VI. 33).

[25]Hense cites Diogenes Laertius VII. 170 here, implying that ἄλλον refers to Cleanthes. Perhaps it did in Metrocles' version, but here the reference seems only a general one.

[26]Cf. Juvenal, *Satire* III. 147ff., especially 149-151: *Si toga sordidula est et rupta calceus alter*
*Pelle patet, vel si consuto vulnere crassum*
*Atque recens linum ostendit non una cicatrix*
Notice that Juvenal makes no reference to nails.

[27]ἵνα appears in Epictetus I. 26, 16 in an exclamation of indignation, and that seems to be the meaning here.

[28]The double (or triple) entendre in ἐλευθέριος defies translation.

[29]Cf. Diogenes Laertius VI. 6 where a similar remark is made about Antisthenes.

[30]γλοιός was the oil and dirt scraped off a person; cf. Teles III.77 and note 21.

[31]There seems to be a mild oxymoron in the words περιχέας and ἐλάδιον: a little oil was enough to pour all around and over the fish.

[32]Cf. Teles II.39ff.

[33]Manes was a slave of Diogenes; cf. Diogenes Laertius VI. 55.

[34]Frag. 201 Edmonds; cf. Horace, *Epistle* I. 12, 10; Seneca, *Consolation to Helvia* 11, 5.

[35]Theognis 109.

[36]With this whole paragraph compare Teles V which concludes with the same Euripidean verses (in a slightly altered form) as appear here in lines 153-154. But the transition into this passage seems abrupt, even for Teles.

[37]Perhaps νῦν δὲ γὰρ should be read in line 149. νῦν refers to his prime, and something is needed to introduce the reason for his dissatisfaction with this stage of life.

[38]ἀβίωτος ὁ βίος is probably a proverb; cf. Teles VII. 113.

[39]Euripides, *Hercules Furens* 637-638. See note 36 above and V.35-36, and note 3.

[40]This proverb seems to appear first with the comic poet Cratinus (cf. frag. 33 Kock). It also appears in Aristotle, *Eth. Nic* I. 6, 16, 1098A18.

[41]Something is wrong with the text here. It may be technically possible to understand σπεύδει κτήσασθαι from line 159, but the intervening proverb (unless it is a parenthetical remark) makes such an ellipsis awkward. This awkwardness extends over the next several phrases, for σπεύδει or some such verb must govern the infinitives there. It is, however, difficult to decide what to do in Teles. Sometimes he repeats over and over (cf. the first selection) even the most non-essential elements of a sentence; sometimes (cf., for example, VII.109ff., 130ff.) he is so elliptical that what remains is almost incomprehensible. Such an inconsistency of style may be the result of the different sources which Teles has used.

[42]Hense defends the δύo of the manuscripts and cites a non-parallel in Galen. But what does δύo modify? The man already wants a δοῦλον ἕτερον. Two swallows? Nonsense. Jacobs' δόμον is palaeographically sound and effectively anticipates ἀγρόν. The only way δύo can be retained is to read εἶτα κἀγρόν, εἶτα δύo.

[43]φυγαδεύειν seems a bit obscure here. This verb can mean either "banish" or "live in banishment." The latter meaning seems out of place here (see lines 172-173), but without an object the verb is vague.

[44]ἀσπανιστία occurs only here.

[45]Frag. 18 (Diels); see Apparatus.

[46]LSJ would have us believe that ἀθώπευτον καὶ ἀκολάκευτον means something like "immune to flattering and
flattery," and so it may in another context.  But such a
thought here is patent nonsense, for there has been no
reference to flattery anywhere in the piece.  LSJ may,
however, provide a clue to the meaning of ἀθώπευτον by
citing its use in Paulus Silèntiarius (Greek Anthology VI.
168,8).  This little poem describes the slaying of a wild
boar, called a θὴρ ἀθώπευτον, which bristles with hair and
is just fresh from its lair.  This description resembles
what we may say of some wandering Cynic preacher.  For a
suitable meaning of ἀκολάκευτον we need go no further than
Plutarch, *On Compliancy* ch. 18, 536A where it means "in-
capable of submission."  Putting these two parallels together and considering the meaning of Teles' passage and
the obvious play on the sense and sound of the words, we
arrive at some such translation as "unkempt and uncom-
promising."

## IVB

[1]For the title of IV, see note IVA. 1.  There may,
however, be three fragments here instead of two.  In line
46 (φασὶ δὲ καὶ) Teles abruptly changes subject.  Up to
this point he has discussed whether wealth or poverty is
more conducive to philosophical activity.  In line 46,
however, the discussion turns to the question of whether
the rich man or the poor man has more honor.  Can it be,
then, that selection IV should be divided into three fragments?  Or can all three be parts of a longer work in
which the several advantages of poverty were contrasted
with the corresponding disadvantages of wealth?  Such a
topic would involve a series of paradoxes in good Cynic
and Stoic fashion.

[2]κωλύει πρὸς τὸ φιλοσοφεῖν is a strange, and possibly unparalleled, construction.  κωλύειν is regularly
transitive, and for that reason Nauck ingeniously proposed
πῶς in place of πρός.  Wilamowitz, however, followed by
Hense, defended the reading of the MSS and cited Thucydides I. 144,2 as an example of the verb's intransitive
use.  Wilamowitz's decision was correct, but his reasoning was wrong.  κωλύειν is transitive in Thucydides, for
the object is readily understood from the previous clause.
The same transitive use of κωλύειν, with the object understood, occurs in Polybius I. 26, 3.  See below, note 6.
A better indication that κωλύει πρὸς τὸ φιλοσοφεῖν is
the correct reading is the remarkably close parallel in
Seneca's *Moral Epistle* 17.3: *multis ad philosophandum
obstitere divitiae; paupertas expedita, secura est.*  Here
*ad philosophandum obstitere* is a close translation of
κωλύει πρὸς τὸ φιλοσοφεῖν, and *obstare ad* is just as
strange in Latin as its counterpart is in Greek.  This
verb regularly requires *quin*, *quominus* or *ne* to introduce

what is being prevented. Thus the similarity of thought in Teles and Seneca plus the same peculiarity of construction point to a common source and to the logical conclusion that the peculiar construction was in the original version.

[3]There is clearly an intended antithesis in σχολάζειν and ἀσχολία. See also the use of εὐσχολώτερος in line 37 (discussed in note 13 below).

[4]Vs. 605.

[5]εὐχερῶς ("cooly," "with indifference"), the reading of the MSS, is strange. εὐκαίρως (see apparatus), seems to fit the context better because of its double meaning of "opportunely" and "in profusion." Other words belonging to this root (e.g., εὔκαιρος, εὐκαιρία) appear in several Stoic passages, and this fact may be an added reason for reading the adverb here.

[6]The construction ἐστὶ πρός + infinitive is rare. LSJ cites only this passage and Polybius I. 26,3: ὄντων δὲ τῶν μὲν πρὸς τὸ κωλύειν τῶν δὲ πρὸς τὸ βιάζεσθαι (sc. τὸν διαπλοῦν). W. R. Paton (in the Loeb edition) translates: "The object of one side being to prevent and that of the other to force a crossing." Perhaps Teles' words should be translated "eager to work."

[7]ζητεῖν seems to have a technical meaning here. Cf., for example, Plato's *Apology* 23B, *Meno* 790; Xenophon's *Mem*. I. 1,15.

[8]The words οὐκ ἔχων τί πράττῃ must mean something like "not knowing what he should do." But such a thought destroys the obvious parallelism in the sentence where οἱ μὲν πλούσιοι is parallel to ὁ δὲ πένης, πλείω πράττοντες to οὐκ ἔχων τί πράττῃ, κωλύονται to γίνεται, and τοῦ σχολάζειν to πρὸς τὸ φιλοσοφεῖν. The proper parallel to πλείω πράττοντες should be something that means "having nothing to do," but the Greek for that is οὐκ ἔχων τι πράττειν. Perhaps that is what should be read here.

[9]Like the construction discussed above in note 6, the combination γίνεσθαι πρός + infinitive is rare, but there is an almost exact parallel in Plato's *Republic* X. 6, 604D1: ἐθίζειν τὴν ψυχὴν ὅτι τάχιστα γίγνεσθαι πρὸς τὸ ἰᾶσθαί τε καὶ ἐπανορθοῦν τὸ πεσόν..., "to accustom the soul as quickly as possible to the healing of the hurt and the raising up of the fallen." Cf. also Stobaeus *Flor*. 93, 31 (Hense, vol. V, p. 762, line 1): καθ᾽ αὑτοὺς μὲν ἄνθρωποι πρὸς ἀρετὴν γεγόνασιν, οὗτος δὲ (sc. ὁ πλοῦτος) ἐφ᾽ αὑτὸν τρέπει. This selection in Stobaeus is one of the two which Gesener identified as another piece by Teles. See Introduction.

[10]For a discussion of this passage, see Ronald F. Hock, "Simon the Shoemaker as an Ideal Cynic," *Greek, Roman and Byzantine Studies*, vol. XVII (1976), pp. 47-53, especially 47ff.

[11]This work is not extant. For a discussion of its contents and importance in antiquity, see A. Lesky (trans. by Willis and de Heer), *A History of Greek Literature*, London[2] 1966, pp. 553-555 and the bibliography listed in the notes.

[12]δόξα may have more than one meaning here. It means "social standing," i.e., the opinion which others have; "political standing," i.e., as king; the "splendor" of his kingly position; and perhaps his "financial standing." No one English word can convey all these nuances.

[13]Despite the definition of εὐσχολώτερος in LSJ and Haines' translation of the word in the Loeb edition of Marcus Aurelius IV. 24, the prefix εὐ- should be given more force. Haines translates εὐσχολώτερος καὶ ἀταρακτό- τερος ἔσται with "he will have more abundant leisure and fret the less." Better is "he will enjoy his leisure more and be less disturbed."

[14]Hense cites Helm, who aptly referred to Lucian's *Gallus* 21 where there is a contrast between the lot of the rich and poor in times of war and peace. But there is nothing in Lucian's passage to explain Teles' νῦν which seems to refer to a specific war. Bevan (loc. cit. p. 85) assumes that the reference is to the Chremonidean war, but if that is true this passage was composed earlier than *On Exile* for Teles refers there (lines III.41ff.) to events that occurred after that war.

[15]The first verse is an accurate quotation of Sophocles' *Oedipus Tyrannus* 62, but the second verse is, as Porson first pointed out, a combination of lines 63-64. Furthermore, the two lines have been combined in such a way that the meaning of 62 has been altered. Lines 63-64 appear like this in Sophocles:
μόνον καθ' αὐτόν, κοὐδεν' ἄλλον· ἡ δ' ἐμὴ
ψυχὴ πόλιν τε κἀμὲ καὶ σ' ὁμοῦ στένει.
Jebb translates the three lines accurately, if not elegantly, with:
Your pain comes on each one of you for himself alone, and for no other: but my soul mourns at once for the city, and for myself, and for thee.
Teles, or his source, would seemingly have made his point more clear and effective if he had quoted the three verses as Sophocles wrote them. As it is, the revision has robbed εἰς ἕν' ἔρχεται, the key phrase of the passage, of most of its meaning, thereby diluting the intended message.

[16]Hense cites Plutarch's *Life of Aristeides* ch. 5, but that passage merely describes how Callias came to be wealthy. Much more to the point are chapters 24-25: 24 relates the events surrounding Aristeides' role as tax-assessor of the Delian League; 25, 3-6 contrasts Aristeides' poverty and Callias' wealth and the reputation each had because of his financial status.

[17]Cf. Plutarch's *Life of Lysander* ch. 30; *Sayings of Spartans* 230A; Aelian, *Varia Historia* VI. 4 and X. 15. It is surprising that Teles did not mention the same dilemma in the case of Aristeides, for whose daughters Athens provided the dowry out of public funds; cf. Plutarch's *Life of Aristeides* ch. 27.

[18]Teles paraphrases *Supplices* 873: νεανίας ἦν τῷ βίῳ μὲν ἐνδεής and quotes 874 except that he changes Euripides' Ἀργείᾳ χθονί to Ἀργείων πόλει. This is a logical sort of change for someone who is quoting from memory, but some texts of Euripides' plays list πόλει as a variant reading and cite Stobaeus (i.e., Teles) as the authority.

## V

[1]The division of man's life into various periods has been a favorite theme in many periods and literatures. Sometimes there are fourteen divisions, sometimes ten, and sometimes (as in Teles) seven. For any English-speaking person the most famous use of this theme occurs in Shakespeare's *As You Like It* (Act II. Sc. vii, lines 139-166). Here, too, seven stages are used, and each corresponds closely to the seven in Teles (but see IVA.146-152 where only four divisions are used).

[2]The statement that man wastes half his life in sleeping appears as early as Aristotle (Nic. Eth. 1102b5). Plutarch (*Whether Fire or Water is More Useful*, ch. 12, 958D) quotes Ariston as making the same statement. This reference to Ariston has been accepted by von Arnim (*S.V.F.I.* p. 90, frag. 403) as a fragment of Ariston of Chios, but why shouldn't the author be the peripatetic philosopher, Ariston of Ceos?

[3]Euripides, *HF* 637-638. See Teles IVA.153-154 where these same words (but with ἀεί added) conclude a similar discussion; cf. IVA, notes 36, 39.

## VI

[1]"Circumstances" may not be the best translation of περιστάσεις. Cf., for example, Epictetus II. 6, 16-17 and Marcus Aurelius IX. 13 where the term clearly means "trouble," "hardships," etc. But Teles seems to take the

word in a neutral sense (cf. line 26 below) in just the way that Epictetus counsels against.

[2]Cf. Teles II.4 for the same image of Fortune.

[3]An hexameter from some unknown poet.

[4]Is there a pun in τυχούσῃ and ἡ τύχη?

[5]Cf. IVA.13-17 and notes 3 and 5.

[6]*Odyssey* I. 191-192.

[7]*Odyssey* I. 194.

[8]Euripides, *Suppl*. 865-866.

[9]Euripides, frag. 892, 4-5 (Nauck), p. 646. This five-line fragment seems to have been a favorite quotation among both Greek and Roman writers. It appears in whole or in part in Athenaeus, Gellius, Sextus Empiricus, Musonius, and four times in Plutarch.

[10]For the same simile, cf. Teles II.67ff. and note II. 17.

[11]It is impossible to retain the pun: τὰ ὅπλα of course means both "arms" and "camp." Since the man is without arms (ψιλός), he must retreat both to camp and to arms. Bevan, op. cit., pp. 87-88 says "to the protection of the heavy troops," but surely Teles would have written εἰς τοὺς ὁπλίτας for that idea. There may also be a pun in ἀναχώρει here and in the next line: "retreat to" and "resort to."

[12]Hense cites as parallels to this idea Philo, *Every Good Man is Free* ch. 6, sect. 34; Marcus Aurelius II. 17; Epictetus III. 24, 34; Seneca, *Moral Epistle* 96, 5.

[13]The traditional garb of the Cynic preacher. There is clearly a progression of sorts in this list, and the effect, especially from a Cynic, seems almost humorous.

## VII

[1]The term ἀπάθεια has had several translations, but in the most recent studies the word "passion" has been used: e.g., Ludwig Edelstein, *The Meaning of Stoicism*, Cambridge, Mass. 1966, pp. 1-4; Helen North, *Sophrosyne*, Ithaca 1966, pp. 215 *et passim*; F. H. Sandbach, *The Stoics*, London 1975, pp. 63-67. On the strength of several ancient passages (notably Epictetus III. 22, 48: οὐκ εἰμι ἄλυπος, οὐκ εἰμι ἄφοβος, οὐκ εἰμι ἐλεύθερος;) "freedom from passion" seems preferable to "absence of passion" or some such neutral idea.

For the ancient controversy over the meaning of ἀπάθεια see the works cited above, and for some ancient representative discussions of the term, see Epictetus I. 4, 28ff; Seneca, *Moral Epistles* 9 and 85; Gellius XII. 5, 10; Philo *Alleg. Inter.* III. 129; Diogenes Laertius V. 31.

[2]For this species of pomegranate, see Theophrastus, *HP* IV. 13, 2, where the plant is said to be shorter-lived than other varieties; Athenaeus (XIV. 650e), who cites a line of Aristophanes (frag. 118 Hall-Geldart); Pliny (*H.N.* XIII.112), who gives a fairly detailed description of the species which he calls *granatum apyrenum* ("seedless seed"); and Seneca (*Moral Epistles* 85,5), who uses the term *Apyrena* (sc. *granata*). Seneca's passage is very similar to that of Teles, and, in fact, the whole epistle should be read along with Teles' selection.

[3]The weary reader must respond in the affirmative.

[4]LSJ defines ἀπερίεργος as "not over-busy," "art-less," "simple" and implies that the word is used only with things. Teles applies it to a person where it clearly has a more pregnant meaning than those given in LSJ. Indeed, it must be the negative of περίεργος in the meaning "officious," "meddlesome," "inquisitive," etc., hence the choice of "incurious." For a discussion of similar topics, cf. Epictetus III. 22, 100ff.

[5]A rare meaning of εὐαρεστέω, but cf. Dion. Hal. XI. 60, 1.

[6]Cf. Seneca, *Moral Epistles* 74, 30.

[7]*Trag. Adesp.* 548, Nauck.

[8]For a good definition of ὠμήν, cf. Sophocles' *Antigone* 471-472: δηλοῖ τὸ γέννημ' ὠμὸν ἐξ ὠμοῦ πατρὸς/ τῆς παιδός· εἴκειν δ' οὐκ ἐπίσταται κακοῖς, i.e., one who does not know how to give in to troubles.

[9]Cf. Plutarch, *Sayings of Spartan Women* 241A and 241D.

[10]The same hysteron proteron occurs in Plutarch's version of the anecdote in 241A.

[11]As Teles gives the story, these words are clearly out of place, for otherwise the syntax of what follows falls apart. Yet it is interesting that Plutarch uses the same words to conclude two different anecdotes. Can it be that in the original version Teles used the same two passages only to have them confused and corrupted by those who transmitted and excerpted his treatise?

94

¹²The words τοῦτο δέ ἐστιν 'ἀπάγξαι' are curious, and
there is, in fact, the temptation to delete them as the
remark of Theodorus or some silly scribe. Hense, however,
gives several references to the use of ἀπάγχω by Cynic
writers (i.e., Antisthenes, Diogenes, Crates) and so these
words may indeed be part of the Cynic version of these
stories. Notice that in Plutarch's account of both stories the mother's final remark is ἢ μὴ ἔσο, i.e., "or don't
live." The Cynic version of these words may well have
been "ἀπάγξαι."

¹³Cf. Plutarch, *op. cit.*, 241C.

¹⁴This repetition of φημί is awkward and unnecessary.
It should probably be deleted.

¹⁵This last sentence is curious and an unnecessary
addition to the anecdote. The fact that it is also pedantic may, however, insure its authenticity. Teles is often
inclined to the pedantic. Yet the phrase ὅτι εὐψύχως is,
despite Hense's defense of such ellipses (pp. XXVIIff.),
uncharacteristically crabbed for Teles, but cf. ἵνα πολυ-
τελῶς, IVA.114.

¹⁶Cf. Plutarch, *op. cit.*, 241B. On the mother's
action, cf. *The Virtues of Women*, 246A, 248B.

¹⁷This is a curious statement for Teles to make if he
was a Megarian. From early times, Megara had been
"Dorized," and despite the city's occasional association
with Athens, Corinth, etc., one would expect Dorian influence to remain strong. Or would such heroics as those
described here have disappeared by Teles' day?

¹⁸As Hense and others have recognized, there is an
obvious lacuna here.

¹⁹Cf. Plutarch, *Life of Pelopidas* ch. 1, 278A; [Plu-
tarch] *Consolation to Apollonius* ch. 15, 110C.

²⁰This is a difficult sentence which can make sense
only by accepting Jacobs' emendation but even so the
thought is rather strange.

²¹Another difficult sentence. I have retained
Meineke's emendation which Hense prints, but I am far from
convinced of its accuracy.

²²Cf. Seneca, *Consolation to Marcia* 16, 7.

²³The combination εἰ ἐάν is remarkable and possibly
unparalleled.

[24]Hense comments on the ellipses in this passage, but they are no more striking than some he has let pass in silence. For the possibility of an even more stringent ellipsis, see note 28 below.

The examples used here are reminiscent of those in *Matt.* 5:29-30, though the context is of course quite different. The *topos* may belong to popular wisdom material.

[25]The usual translation of μαργίτης, which should probably be printed as a proper name.

[26]This is the first of several related problems which resist solution. Something is needed here to govern the two infinitives, and Buecheler's εἰκός, which Hense prints, is a good suggestion and palaeographically sound, for it could easily have fallen out after γυναικός. But what verb are we to understand: εἶ or ἐστι?

[27]The manuscripts have εἰ...ἀπέθανε, παρεκάλεσεν (or παρεκάλεις)ἄν, and this is what Hense prints. If we follow the manuscripts, the subject of this clause, as well as the preceding one, is third person; if we follow Meineke (yet the mixture of aorist and imperfect is unusual), the subject of both clauses is second person. There is no doubt that the subject of the following section is second person, as οἴει proves.

[28]Hense gave up on the phrase ἀλλ' οὐ πρᾴως καὶ εἴπερ ἕτερον, but some sense can be made of these words. There are two possibilities: 1) assume an outrageous amount of ellipsis and understand these words to represent something like this: ἀλλ' οὐ οἴει δεῖν πρᾴως φέρειν καὶ ἴει ἕτερον δεῖν πρᾴως φέρειν ("But you feel that you need not bear the misfortune calmly even if you feel another man should bear them calmly"). Naturally no writer would spell out the thought to that extent, but this expansion gives one possible interpretation of Teles' thought. 2) A second possibility is to retain ἀλλ' οὐ πρᾴως (an earlier writer would probably have added μήν. Cf. J. D. Denniston, *The Greek Particles*, Oxford 1934, p. 345) with what goes before and put καὶ εἴπερ ἕτερον with the next sentence. There is still the need for supposing an ellipsis, for οἴει δεῖν is still needed. The meaning is "...and not calmly at that; and you feel that if another man is distressed you should advise...." Either possibility gives a sense that is adequate and in keeping with the general thought of the whole passage.

[29]Without some such word as οἴει understood (as suggested in note 28 above) παρακαλεῖν has nothing on which to depend, and without ἕτερον the adjective μέτριον (sc. εἶναι) has nothing to modify. Hense suggests that we understand μέτριον as μετριάζοντα, but this meaning seems unparalleled and does not remove the need for a noun.

[30]By his punctuation, Hense seems to take both
ἀντιθέναι and ἐξισοῦν with what goes before, thus leaving
the words ἀπογέγονε ὁ φίλος, καὶ γὰρ γέγονε isolated and
dangling.  It seems necessary to take ἀντιθέναι with what
goes before and ἐξισοῦν with what follows.  Then, since
ἐξισοῦν implies two things, we need to change Hense's
punctuation and read 'ἀπογέγονε ὁ φίλος' 'καὶ γὰρ γέγονε.'
There is a temptation to suggest the insertion of another
καὶ between the two quotations, but it is not really
necessary.  But that the two parts of this saying are to
be balanced seems clear not only from the meaning of the
infinitive ἐξισοῦν but from the assonance and the untranslatable play on the meanings of ἀπογέγονε and γέγονε.

[31]Cf. Seneca, *Moral Epistle* 77,11.

[32]This passage is very unsatisfactory.  The second
person is an emendation of Jacobs, but the third person of
the manuscripts may be better.  Neither reading, however,
makes the sense clear, nor does it tie the thought closely
enough with the remark of Socrates which follows.

[33]Cf. Xenophon, *Memorabilia* I. 1, 18.  For a similar
idea, cf. Juvenal VI. 592ff. and especially III. 350-353.

[34]As Hense and others have seen, the passage is based
on that of Xenophon with, perhaps, some intermediary versions.  But once again Teles' account is so elliptical
that it is all but incomprehensible without Xenophon's
version as a guide.  Jacobs (see Hense's apparatus) has
suggested filling in all the omitted words, but he has
gone too far.  Both Jacobs and Hense seem not to have
realized that πλείω is a noun here, and the fact that it
is a noun removes the necessity of adding anything to the
text except the two participles, without which the two oc-
currences of τῷ are nonsense.

[35]The thought of this sentence follows very closely
upon that expressed in line 126.  This fact adds to the
awkwardness of lines 127-129 discussed in note 32 above.

[36]With the passage that follows, cf. Plutarch, *Stoic
Self-Contradictions* ch. 2, 1033B-C and Cherniss' notes in
the Loeb edition, vol. XIII B, pp. 414-415.  In his attack
on Zeno, Cleanthes, and Chrysippus Plutarch asserts that
in the life of none of them can one find στρατηγίαν,
νομοθεσίαν, πάροδον εἰς βουλήν, συνηγορίαν ἐπὶ δικαστῶν,
στρατείαν ὑπὲρ πατρίδος, πρεσβείαν, or ἐπίδοσιν.  The list
is more elaborate than Teles', but the two seem somehow to
be related.

[37]The logic of ἱερεύοντος is dubious.  Why should one
lose a friend because he is sacrificing?  Are we to understand that the friend has gone abroad for this purpose?
Perhaps we should read ἱερατεύοντος ("when he becomes a

priest"), but again this activity would not explain the loss of a friend unless the service were abroad, for men who held priesthoods were not cut off from other activities and certainly not from family and friends.

But perhaps we need not look for logic here. Notice what follows: why should either illness or old age deprive one of friends. Indeed, the show of friendship at such times is a recurring theme in friendship literature.

[38]This phrase makes no sense unless we are to understand that it depends upon ἡγεῖσθαι, and even then the thought is vague.

[39]J. D. Denniston (*The Greek Particles*, Oxford 1934, p. 442) says that the phrase ἀλλ᾽ οὖν γε "can hardly stand in classical Greek." He does, however, cite Isocrates XX. 14, Lycurgus 141 (in both of which he approves of emendations that remove γε), and pseudo-Aristotle *De Mundo* 397b12 which he defends as post-classical. Perhaps he should have included these two uses of Teles.

[40]Cf. Seneca, *Moral Epistle* 85,33: *Neptune, numquam hanc navem nisi rectam*. Both the Greek and Latin versions are elliptical and require us to understand some verb meaning "sink" or "destroy."

[41]Hense believes that the selection has a satisfactory conclusion and cites Seneca, *Moral Epistle* 98,14 as a parallel. Yet this *Epistle* has another four sections and it is Hense who first suggested that it end with section 14, thus making the rest a fragment of another epistle. See R. M. Gummere (in the Loeb edition, p. 126), who, however, agrees with Hense.